AQUARIUM

David Vann

Atlantic Monthly Press
New York

Copyright © 2015 by David Vann

Published simultaneously in Canada
Printed in the United States of America

FIRST EDITION

ISBN 978-0-8021-2352-7
eISBN 978-0-8021-9175-5

Atlantic Monthly Press
an imprint of Grove/Atlantic, Inc.
154 West 14th Street
New York, NY 10011

Distributed by Publishers Group West

www.groveatlantic.com

15 16 17 18   10 9 8 7 6 5 4 3 2

For my good and generous mother, Lorraine Ida Vann

It was a fish so ugly it didn't seem to be a fish at all. A rock made of cold flesh mossy and overgrown, mottled green and white. I hadn't seen it at first, but then I pressed my face to the glass and tried to get closer. Buried in that impossible growth, the curve downward of thick lips, grimace for a mouth. Small black bead of an eye. Thick tail banded with dark spots. But nothing else recognizable as fish.

He's an ugly one.

An old man next to me suddenly, his voice an unwelcome surprise. No one ever spoke to me here. Dark rooms, humid and warm, haven from the snow outside.

I guess so, I said.

Those eggs. He's keeping them all safe.

And then I saw the eggs. I had thought the fish was partially hidden behind a white sea anemone, a clump of rounded soft white orbs, but I could see now there were no stalks, each orb individual, eggs somehow hanging together on the side of this fish.

Three-spot frogfish, the man said. They don't know why the male keeps the eggs. Could be to keep them safe. Could be to lure other fish near.

Where are the three spots?

The old man chuckled. Good point. More spots on him than on an old man's hand.

I didn't look. I didn't want to see his hand. He was very old, as in almost dead. At least seventy or something but standing okay. His breath an old person's breath. I cupped my hands at the glass and moved away a bit, as if I were just looking for a better viewing angle.

How old are you? he asked.

Twelve.

You're a pretty girl. Why aren't you with your friends, or your mother?

My mother works. I wait for her here. She picks me up at four thirty or five, depending on traffic.

Just then the fish lifted a fin partway, exactly like toes peeling away from rock, soft pale underside.

Our legs and arms are fins, I said. Look at his. Almost like toes grabbing the rock.

Wow, the old man said. We've changed so much we no longer recognize ourselves.

I looked at him then, the old man. Mottled flesh like the fish, hair hanging over in a part the way this fish's upper fin curled over the eggs. Mouth in a grimace, lips downward. Small eyes buried in puffy lined flesh, camouflage, looking away. He was afraid.

Why are you here? I asked.

I just want to see. I don't have much time.

Well you can watch the fish with me.

Thank you.

The frogfish wasn't floating above the rocks. He was clinging to them. He looked like he would flee at any moment, but he hadn't moved except to readjust his toes.

I bet it's warm in there, the man said. Tropical water. Indonesia. A whole life spent surrounded by warm water.

Like never getting out of the bath.

Exactly.

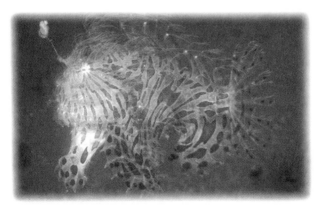

Another strange fish floated by higher above us, like leopard-print lace with the spots stretched. See-through fins and no shape of a fish, only a splotch of pattern.

Striated frogfish, the man said. A relative. Its Latin name mentions the antenna.

Where's his mouth, or his eye, or anything?

I don't know.

How can they even call that a fish?

It's a good question.

How old are you?

The man grinned. Sounds like you're questioning how I can even be called a human.

Sorry.

It's okay. I have to admit, I wonder about this myself. If I can hardly walk, and I'm alone, and I'm no longer recognizable, my face nothing like it was before, all the parts of it hiding away, so that I'm a surprise even to myself, then can you call that what you called it before? Isn't it something new? And if no one else sees it, is it anything?

I'm sorry.

No. It's an interesting question, one we should think about together. It would be my pleasure. We can think about whether he's a fish and I'm a human.

Well I have to go. It's almost four thirty, so my mother might drive up.

What time will you be here tomorrow?

School's out at two forty. So about quarter after three.

Where do you go to school?

Gatzert.

Isn't that a long way to walk?

Yeah. Okay bye. I walked away in a hurry through those dark corridors rimmed in light. The aquarium itself felt like it was underwater, a submarine at tremendous depth.

And then I'd emerge into the lobby and suddenly it was another world, the bright clouds of a Seattle sunset, a few orange patches in gray, streets wet. Snow turned to black and brown slush, waiting to become ice. My mother not yet at the curb.

I put my coat on and zipped up. I loved the feel of being doubled in size. I pulled the hood over my head, fake fur. I was almost invisible.

My mother rarely showed up at four thirty. I always started waiting then, but I had a lot of time to look at the railroad tracks across the street and the freeway overpasses beyond. Great slabs of dark concrete in the sky, the world banded. You could go north or south from here, and we always went south. The street was called Alaskan Way, but we never went that way.

Trucks and endless cars, concrete and sound and cold, nothing like the world of fish. They had never felt wind. They had never been cold or seen snow. But they did have to wait. All they did was wait. And what did they see in the glass? Did they see us, or only reflections of themselves, a house of mirrors?

I was going to be an ichthyologist when I grew up. I was going to live in Australia or Indonesia or Belize or on the Red Sea and spend most of my day submerged in that same warm water. A fish tank stretching thousands of miles. The problem with the aquarium was that we couldn't join them.

My mother drove an old Thunderbird. Apparently she had imagined a freer life before I came along. The front hood was half the length of the car. An enormous engine that galloped high and low at the curb. It could die at any moment, but it was going to finish off all the gas in the world first.

Two-tone brown paint, lighter along the sides of the car, peeling all across the hood and roof, like galaxies opening up, silver suns in clusters too far away to name.

The door swung wide like the counterweight for a crane, thousands of pounds. I always had to pull with both hands to try to bring it back.

How were the fish?

Okay.

Make any friends? This was my mother's joke almost every day, about my making friends with the fish. I wasn't going to tell her that today I actually had made a friend.

I finally got the door closed, and we sputtered off. We didn't wear seat belts.

My mother worked in the container port, basic labor. She wore heavy work boots, brown Carhartt overalls, a flannel shirt, her hair back in a ponytail. But she was starting to do some rigging of cranes and hoped someday to be a crane operator. They made a lot of money, sometimes over a hundred thousand. We'd be rich.

How was school?

Okay. Mr. Gustafson said next year our grades will matter.

And they don't now?

No. He said sixth grade doesn't matter. But seventh grade matters a little bit. He said nothing really matters until eighth grade, but seventh matters a little.

God, where do they find these people? And it's supposed to be a better school. I had to lie about our address to get you in up there.

I like Mr. Gustafson.

Oh yeah?

He's funny. He can never find anything. Today we all had to look for one of his books.

Well that's a great recommendation. I take back everything I said.

Ha, I said, to show I understood. I was looking at all the graffiti, as I usually did. On the rail cars and walls, fences and old buildings. The artists made sequences, like flip books. MOE in bright green and blue, tubular, heading uphill, cresting next in orange and yellow, sinking in gold and red, rising again in blue-black, endless path of the sun. The city something that had to be viewed at speed, but we were always locked in traffic. Five and a half miles from the aquarium to our apartment, but it could take half an hour.

Alaskan Way became East Marginal Way South, which was not as romantic. Hard to dream of going there. If our ride home were a cruise, one of the stops would be Northwest Glacier, which was not ice falling in great slabs but ready-mix concrete, sand, and gravel in great bays and silos chalked white.

We lived next to Boeing Field, an airport but not one used to go anywhere. We were in the flight path of all the test planes that might or might not work. The businesses in our area were the Sawdust Supply, tire centers, Army Navy Surplus, Taco Time, tractor and diaper services, rubber and burgers and lighting systems. On most sides of us, you'd find concrete only, stretching for several miles, no trees, enormous parking lots, used and unused, but you wouldn't know that when you arrived at our apartment. We looked out on the parking lots of the Transportation Department, endlessly shifting stacks of orange highway cones and barrels, yellow crash barriers, moveable concrete dividers, trucks of all kinds, but the eight buildings of our apartment complex had trees all around and looked as nice as what you'd find in a rich section of town. Subsidized housing with bay windows, pastel colors, pretty wooden fences with latticework. And constantly patrolled by police.

The moment we arrived home, my mother always collapsed on her bed with a big sigh, and she let me collapse on top of her. Cigarette smell in her hair, though she didn't smoke. Smell of hydraulic fluid. The soft strong mountain of her underneath me.

Bed, she said. I'd like to never leave bed. I love the bed.

Like *Willy Wonka and the Chocolate Factory*.

That's right. We'll have our heads at opposite ends and just live right here.

I had my hands up under her armpits and my feet slid under her thighs, locked on. No frogfish ever gripped a rock as tightly. This apartment our own aquarium.

Your old mother has a date tonight.

No.

Yeah, sorry salamander.

What time?

Seven. And you'll need to sleep in your room, in case your mother gets lucky.

You don't even like them.

I know. That's usually the case. But who knows. There's a nice man out there every once in a while.

What's his name?

Steve. He plays harmonica.

Is that his job?

My mother laughed. You imagine a better world, sweet pea.

How did you meet him?

He works in IT, fixing computer systems, and came to fix something at work. He was around at lunch, playing Summertime on his harmonica, so I ate lunch with him.

Do I get to meet him?

Sure. But we need to have dinner first. What do you want?

Sink dogs?

My mother laughed again. I closed my eyes and rode her back as it rose and fell.

But finally my mother rolled over, as she always did, crushing me to get me to let go. I'd never let go until there was no breath left, then I'd tap out against her shoulder like a Big Time wrestler.

Shower time, she said.

Steve did not look like a computer guy. He was strong, like my mother. Big shoulders. Both of them wearing dark flannel shirts and jeans.

Hello there, he said to me, so cheery I couldn't help smiling, even though I had planned to be mean to him. You must be Caitlin. I'm Steve.

You play harmonica?

Steve smiled like he had been caught with a secret. He had a dark moustache, and that made him seem like a magician. He pulled a silver harmonica out of his shirt pocket and held it out for me to see.

Play something.

What would you like?

Something fun.

A sea shanty, then, he said in a pirate voice. And we can kick up our heels a bit. He played something from a ship, merry but slow at first, kicking out one toe and then another and turning and speeding up as my mother and I joined, linking our arms, and then he was hopping and frog-legging all around our living room and I was going mad with joy, shouting and my mother shushing me but smiling. An unconscious child-joy that could explode like the sun, and I wanted Steve to stay with us forever.

But they left on their date, left me sweaty and wound up and with nothing to do, pacing around the apartment.

I hated when my mother left me alone. Sometimes I read a book, or watched TV. I wanted a fish tank, but they cost too much and weren't allowed because they might break and flood the apartment below through the floor and do thousands of dollars in damage. Nothing was alive in our apartment. Bare white walls, low ceilings, bare lights, so lonely when my mother was gone. Time something that nearly stopped. I sat down on the floor against a wall, gray carpet extending, and listened to the wires in the light above. I hadn't even asked him what his favorite fish was. I asked everyone that.

I found the old man peering in so close it looked like he was being sucked into the tank. Mouth open and eyes unbelieving.

Handfish, he said. Red handfish. Even less like fins than the frogfish yesterday.

It was a tall narrow tank for sea horses, slim columns of seaweed for them to ride. But at the bottom, in dark rock, was a small cave, pearled around its edges by something mineral in its shine, golden, and guarding the entrance were two pink polka-dotted fish painted red on their lips like children first trying lipstick, exactly what I looked like when I first tried, the red smeared beyond every edge.

Look at him, the old man said. Like he's leaning out a window.

It was true. Hands painted bright red like the lips, and one of the fish had a hand down on the sill, his other up on the side, as if the cave were a window and he was grabbing on to lean out and take a closer look at us. Small bright red eye, looking wary, and a red nose hung upward on a stalk. Some red whiskers hanging down and red along the tip of his dorsal fin, the ridge of his back, but only these few accents, like a clown wearing a pink nightie. His wife in front of the cave, resting on their purple lawn, strange sea grass.

What are the golden pearls? I asked. Are those eggs?

I see what you mean. I think so. I think they're guarding eggs, and we look like we might want to steal a couple.

I've already had lunch.

The old man laughed. Well, I'll be sure to let them know.

The handfish opened his mouth, as if he might say something, then closed it again. His elbows flexed at the windowsill.

It doesn't look like they have scales, I said. They look sweaty.

Up all night, the old man said. Guarding the eggs. Those sea horses are not to be trusted.

We looked up pale green fronds to where the sea horses hung uneasily, pitched unlevel. Bodies of armor assembled in layers, made of something like bone. Not meant to swim.

What's the point of sea horses? I asked.

The old man stood before them, mouth hung open, as if before his god. I remember he looked like that. So unlike any other adult I knew. His mind wasn't on a track. He was ready to be surprised and stopped at any moment, ready to see what would happen next, and it could be anything.

I think there's no answer to that, he finally said. Those are the best questions, the ones that have no answers. I can't imagine how sea horses could have come to be, and why they have heads like horses on land, why there'd be that symmetry unknown. No horse will ever see a sea horse, or a sea horse a horse, and nothing else might ever have recognized both of them, and even though we do recognize the symmetry now, what's the point? That's exactly the right kind of question.

Are they made of bone, all those ridges?

The old man looked at the written descriptions beside the tank. Let's see. Hey, they're telling us here to look for pygmy sea horses, on the gorgonian coral. Should be red and white.

Both of us leaned closer. Above the handfish cave were branches of coral dusted pale white with pink warts, but no sea horses.

I don't see anything, I said. Just coral.

They're only two centimeters long, he said.

That's tiny.

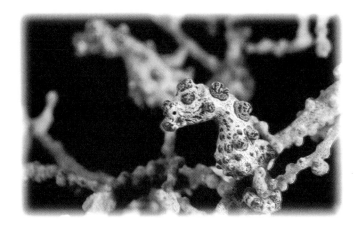

And then I saw it. Warts too pink, too bright and clean, not dusted pale. Double wrap of the tiniest tail around a branch, like a miniature snake made of glass. The rounded belly and horse's head and the smallest black dot of an eye, and covered in these pink mounds just like the coral.

I found one, I said. Then I noticed the shadow beyond, a second pygmy sea horse in exactly the same position, as if all things must be doubled in order to exist.

Where? he asked, but I couldn't speak.

Ah, he said. I see it now.

A shadow self, not made of flesh. Brittle as the coral. Hanging in a void. Already one of these sea horses was mine, known, and the other was other.

I don't like the second one, I said. The second one gives me the creeps.

Why? He looks pretty much the same. Or she, or whatever. How can you tell male or female?

I can't stay here.

Living things made of stone. No movement. And a terrifying loss of scale, the world able to expand and contract. That tiny black pinprick of an eye the only way in, opening to some other larger universe.

I walked away quickly, past tank after tank of pressure magnified and color dimmed, shape distorted. They had speakers for the tanks, and at the moment it was all too much, the parrot fish tearing at coral and shrimp clicking, chittering of penguins. Sound increased beyond measure, the shifting of a few grains of sand like boulders.

I stopped at the largest tank, an entire wall of dim pale blue, reassuring, no sound. Slow movement of sharks, same movement for a hundred million years. The sharks like monks, repetition of days, endless circling, no desire for more but only this movement. Eyes going opaque, no longer needing to see. No fancy clothes but hung in gray with white beneath. Viewed from above, they could look like the ocean floor. Viewed from below, they could look like the sky.

What's wrong? the old man asked. He was kneeling beside me. He was kind.

I don't know, I said. And this was true. I had no idea. Just some childhood panic in me, and I think now it was because I had only my mother. I had one person in this world, and she was everything, and somehow that shadow-shape, that doubling in the tank of coral, made me feel how easy she'd be to lose. I had nightmares all the time in which she was underneath a crane in the port and one of those huge containers flying through the air above her. We know fish are always on guard, hiding at the mouth of a cave or in seaweed or clung to coral, trying to look invisible. Their ends could come from anywhere, at any time, a larger mouth out of the dark and all instantly gone. But aren't we the same? A car accident at any moment, a heart attack, disease, one of those containers coming loose and falling through the sky, my mother below not even looking up, seeing and feeling nothing, just the end.

The old man put a hand on my shoulder. You're okay, he said. You're safe.

I do remember he said that. He said I was safe. He always said exactly the right thing. I gave him a hug then, my arms wrapped around his neck. I needed someone to hold on to. Hair dry as grass, bones in his shoulders, nothing soft, as armored as a sea horse and as ugly, but I clung to him like my own branch of coral.

My mother that evening was tired. She lay on the couch and I snugged against her and we watched TV, mostly commercials. Back in our aquarium, as territorial and easily found as any fish. We had only four places to hide in this tank: the couch, the bed, the table, and the bathroom. If you checked those four spots, you'd always find us. The bare white walls gone blue in the light from the TV, no different from glass. A ceiling clamped down above so we couldn't jump out and escape. Sound of a filter and pump running, the heating unit, keeping us at the right temperature. The only question was who was outside, looking in.

Are you going to marry Steve?

Whoa. Slow down there, cowgirl.

But you like him?

Yes. Yes I do.

So why not marry him?

I turned to look at my mother, and she was studying me, too.

You're wanting a father?

I didn't answer. We had talked about this before, and I always got in trouble somehow.

Look, she said. There's something that adults call expectations, which means that we never get what we want and in fact we don't get it because we want it. So the way it works is that if I really want Steve, if I want to marry him, then he runs away. If I don't want him, then he'll keep coming around and we won't be able to get rid of him. And this will be even more true for you, because being a father is a much bigger thing than being a husband. So if you want Steve to be your father, he'll run. But if you can just enjoy Steve because he's fun, maybe he'll stick around for a bit.

That doesn't make any sense.

That's true. It doesn't make any sense. Welcome to the adult world, coming soon. I work so I can work more. I try not to want anything so maybe I'll get something. I starve so I can be less and more. I try to be free so I can be alone. And there's no point to any of it. They left out that part.

Who's they?

The evil little gremlins who run the world. Who knows. Don't make me talk about this stuff. Just watch TV. I'm tired.

Sorry.

It's okay. It's not your fault. Don't let me ever make you feel that any of the problems in my life are your fault. They're not.

Okay.

My mother rarely spoke like this. I wanted to fix the world for her, make it all make sense. She was good and strong and should have been given everything. She kissed the top of my head and pulled me closer and I burrowed in.

I didn't watch the TV. I watched the walls, the flickering light. Somehow all colors became shades of blue, as if the air really were water. And why weren't all fish blue, in a range dimming from white-blue to blue-black as they went deeper? Why were any fish bright yellow, or red? They were all hiding, so why these bright flashes and patterns?

Where did you grow up?

Caitlin. You know I don't like to think about any of it.

But you never say anything.

That's right.

But it was here in Seattle?

Yes.

And was it a room like this?

No. I mean maybe it was the same kind of room, but what matters is who's in a room, or who's not there, not the room itself. Although the room itself wasn't anything like this either.

Well tell me.

No.

Why not?

Because it's enough that they wrecked my life. They don't get to touch yours.

But what happened?

Caitlin.

Okay.

We had no family. No one at all. Everyone at school had a family. They didn't have fathers, many of them, but they did have aunts and uncles and grandparents and cousins. And almost all fish were in more than pairs. Although as I thought about it, many of the fish in the aquarium were in fact in pairs or alone, and how could that be? It couldn't be like that in the ocean.

The entire planet one ocean. I liked to think about this. When I went to sleep each night, I imagined myself at the bottom, thousands of feet down, the weight of all that water but I was gliding just above ground, something like a manta ray, flying soundless and weightless over endless plains that fell away into deep canyons of darker black and then rose up in spires and new plateaus, and I could be anywhere in this world, off Mexico or Guam or under the Arctic or all the way to Africa, all in the one element, all home, shadows on all sides of me gliding also, great wings without sound or sight but felt and known.

Mr. Gustafson had us all preparing for Christmas. There was a great confusion about this, because we were also preparing for Hanukkah and Chinese New Year and Diwali and something in Korea, but the dates weren't the same and we all knew we were really preparing for Christmas without being able to say it. Everything was red and green and said Happy Holidays. This was our last year of grades that didn't matter, so we were still free to work on art projects.

I was working on a paper-mache reindeer with Shalini, who was from New Delhi, so we were making it a Diwali reindeer, even though Diwali had already passed a month ago on November 3. It was a different date every year according to the moon.

Add more water to the paste, Shalini said. She was bossy.

Our reindeer was a goddess named Lakshmi Rudolph and wore a hat we were going to paint gold. She was going to make everyone rich and beautiful whether the other reindeer allowed it or not. She would still have a red nose but maybe not any horns, which were difficult anyway in paper-mache.

Shalini had a scarf that was gold, and I was intensely jealous. She had delicious lunches in Tupperware from home, but I had to eat the school lunch. Tater tots almost every day, steamed vegetables, and some kind of meat with gravy, even though I didn't like meat. I was going to be a vegetarian like Shalini when I got older, and I never ate fish.

Shalini was also allowed to wear perfume, which my mother said was ridiculous for twelve-year-olds.

Let me smell your wrists, I said.

You always ask for that.

I like it.

She lifted a wrist for me. Her smooth, beautiful brown arm, and I put my nose against her wrist and closed my eyes and breathed in another world. Things I couldn't name, spicy and sweet.

Your mother should let you wear perfume.

She won't.

Let's keep moving, Caitlin and Shalini, Mr. Gustafson said. Rudolph has no legs.

Lakshmi Rudolph, I said, but Mr. Gustafson had already moved on to the sleigh.

Shalini scrunched her nose to make a pig face. She always said Mr. Gustafson looked like a pig, and it's true the end of his nose did seem cut short a bit, so you could see the dark holes of his nostrils. But every teacher in school was named after an animal. Mr. Callahan was named badger, Miss Martinez was called turtle. None of them were named after fish.

Lakshmi Rudolph had a thin chest still, and bare wire legs, but her head and crown looked good, and her butt and small tail, which we were going to paint white at the tip. Shalini was working on the ribs.

Tell me more about your family, I said.

You always ask about my family.

Tell me more about the wedding, with two elephants and many days and hundreds of people.

That was in India. You should come to my house for a sleepover.

Yay!

Okay. I'll ask my mother.

There was almost no snow left outside. Everything soaked, every patch of lawn swelled, slush in the gutters, ribbons of black. Even the pavement and buildings looked fat with water. Clouds bending downward, gray and darker gray, nothing white. I was one of the only walkers. Everyone drove.

East Yesler Way didn't seem like it was in a city. Lined with two-story apartment complexes, with front yards that looked like backyards, some of them littered with plastic toys and laundry and thrown-away furniture but most looking tidy enough behind their chain-link fences. Smokers standing in the cold, watching me pass. Maybe it did look like a city. Just not downtown, even though we were close.

Almost every day someone was moving in or out. And they could be anyone, any race or age, with or without kids. Like one big motel, that entire long street, built for no one's dream. I didn't like East Yesler Way because no one belonged, but for some reason I never walked down one of the other streets. I had a pathway, a route, as unthinking as the sharks that circled like monks. I felt safe, at least, in my big jacket, and no one bothered me, which I find amazing when I look back on it now. I Google the street and see the crime rate at three times the national average, car theft almost six times higher. I think of my mother and the teachers at school letting me walk that route every day, and I'm filled with a rage that will never go away because it comes from some hollow vertigo unfinished. I feel dizzy with fear for my former self, and how can that be? I'm here now. I'm safe. I have a job. I'm thirty-two years old. I live in a better section of town. I should forgive and forget.

The only thing that kept me moving along that street each afternoon was the blue at the end, the sea visible because we were on a hill. That blue promised the aquarium. A gauntlet leading to a sanctuary. I could have stayed in an after-school program, but it was my choice to visit the fish. They were emissaries sent from a larger world. They were the same as possibility, a kind of promise.

When I crossed over the freeway, downtown began. The hill slanting downward, large buildings shaped like wedges burrowed into the hill, hiding in their own caves. Hunched for safety, as if something enormous swam in the skies above. One brave skyscraper at the end with a pointy top, trying not to look soft. The entire city a colony like coral, made of an endless network of small chambers. I imagined each room a polyp, a creature without a spine, tentacled mouth looking up toward the sky, finding a place to sit and excreting its exoskeleton, a thin layer of concrete, to attach itself here forever, at each full moon waving its tentacles upward and releasing gametes, fairy creatures made of light, each of them a new room floating through the air, looking for a place to build itself.

And so the city would grow without end, but why here? This was no Bali or Belize. Cold, raining all the time, windy, overcast, and dark. Seattle never made sense to me. We had orcas, and beautiful islands I had never seen, called the San Juans, but why the city?

I walked along the ferry terminal, the large green and white ferries that went to these islands, and I wished my mother was free and had money and we could ride north on the water. We would never stop but would just keep voyaging all over the world, across to Japan and down to the Philippines, from island to island, learning to dive, visiting every reef.

I passed fireboats and private yachts, the same private yachts that were always at the dock, never used, always waiting, owned by people with money who never left either, caught somewhere in the city. The waterfront park and then the aquarium. I had a yearly pass, but they all recognized me here and I never had to show it. I just walked in, as if it were my home.

I found him at the darkest tank, in a corner, alone, peering through what could have been a window to the stars, endless black and cold and only a few points of light. Hung in this void like a small constellation, the ghost pipefish, impossible.

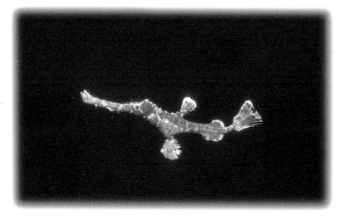

Like a leaf giving birth to stars, I said, whispering, as if any sound might make the fish vanish.

Yes, the old man whispered back. Exactly that. I couldn't have said it better myself. Sometimes I can't believe you're only twelve. You should become an ichthyologist. This is who you are.

Body of small green leaves, veined, very thin, its fins painted in light cast from elsewhere, but from his eye out his long snout, an eruption of galaxies without foreign source, born in the fish itself. An opening in the small fabric of the world, a place to fall into endlessly.

He's my favorite fish, I said, still whispering. I ask everyone what their favorite fish is, and I always hope they'll say the ghost pipefish.

Well he's my favorite now, because of what you've said. The old man looked up at the signs above the tank. Randall Halimeda Ghost Pipefish.

A light flutter of fins, and the fish turned away, became nearly invisible, so thin, suspended in nothing. Some days I waited here and never saw him, only a black tank nearly empty, a dark wall of rock in shadow, a few drab seaweeds along the bottom, camouflage he never used, as if he knew all was staged and no predator coming. This tank could seem like nothing, and then it could dazzle.

Well, the old man said. You see that and it's hard to care about the others. And I have to say, I'm surprised at how many fish here don't look like fish. A leaf giving birth to stars is exactly right, and you'd never see that on your plate.

I don't eat fish, I said.

No, no. I shouldn't either. I'll stop.

I love them too much.

Yes.

What was your favorite fish until today?

I come from Louisiana. Long ago. And they have giant catfish there, fish you wouldn't believe, living down in the mud. They'd never get one in this aquarium. The real world is too big.

What do they look like? I've only seen regular catfish, and small tropical ones from the Amazon, white with black spots.

These are plain. Dark backs, black or brown, rough-looking with some spots, but no regular pattern. White bellies, an obscene white like fat. They look almost like tadpoles, baby frogs, because the belly is so big and rounded and the rest of the body in one long slab, much slimmer. And it doesn't look like flesh. It looks like yuck, like whatever makes frog. But it's hundreds of pounds, longer than a person and much thicker. With stubby little front fins like arms that didn't grow. Long white tendrils around a big hole of a mouth.

It sounds awful. Why is it your favorite?

Because they make dinosaurs possible. If you look long enough at a catfish that big, and think of it lying around in a shallow muddy river, you can imagine the huge leg of a dinosaur stepping into that river. You can go back a hundred million or two hundred million years and touch the world before we existed. Those catfish are leftovers.

I want to see one.

Well maybe someday we'll go to Louisiana together.

I want to go now.

Me too. We could travel and see a lot together. Mexico, maybe, and see manta rays doing backflips.

Really?

Yeah. They leap out of the water there, doing backward somersaults. You wouldn't believe it. Huge manta rays, and you can see fifty of them, or a hundred, all at one time. The Sea of Cortez.

Promise you'll take me there.

I will.

Steve came to dinner, his harmonica in his T-shirt pocket. I was waiting for him to play, but my mother had made me promise to behave and not ask for anything. Think of yourself as a barnacle, she had said. You are a barnacle, just enjoying the water and maybe collecting a little plankton, but not moving or asking anything.

So I sat glued to my chair, encased in my calcium carbonate shell, and I had my small fan out, waving in the current, ready to collect anything interesting, but so far it was boring adult talk about nothing.

We were having hamburgers, my mother's specialty. She mixed green onions with the ground beef, several eggs and bacon bits. That was the hidden bacon. Then she had big strips of bacon across the tops of the burgers, and a lot of barbeque sauce. Potato salad on the side, and barbeque chips and pickles, orange soda. She called it picnic dinner, and I was savoring every bite because I would be a vegetarian soon.

Steve was jolly. He wasn't fat, like most jolly people, but he'd sort of shake up and down in his chair laughing as if he were fat. And what my mother was saying wasn't even funny. He'd bring his napkin up to his mouth with both hands to wipe the barbeque sauce, even though it was only a small paper napkin, and when he did this, you could see how big his biceps were. He was wearing a black T-shirt that had nothing on it. Just these big veined biceps bulging under pressure and then relaxing again.

What's your favorite fish? I blurted out finally. There was no easy way to do it. They were going to talk all night without me.

Caitlin, my mother said.

It's okay, Steve said. Favorite fish. There are so many. Your mother says you go to the aquarium every day.

I do.

What's your favorite fish there?

I asked you first.

Steve leaned back and did his jolly bouncing chuckle. It's been a while since I've heard that, he said. That brings me right back to the playground.

Well?

Okay, he said. I worked on fishing boats in Alaska a few summers, and my favorite fish was the halibut.

I like halibut.

They're pretty cool.

So why are they your favorite?

My mother nudged my foot under the table and then gave me a look. Think barnacle, she said.

Come on, I said. Tell me.

Okay. I like them because they have both eyes on one side of their head, both resting on top and the other side of their face is blind, without eyes, always buried in silt or mud, faced downward into nothing. I like that blind side to them, the idea of it. It says something about us, I think.

So deep, my mother said, and threw a balled-up napkin at him.

I like that, I said.

Halibut used to be my favorite for a different reason, Steve said. I used to think they started with one eye on each side of their head. Swimming along normally, like any other fish, like a salmon. But then they hit puberty, and one eye migrated over to the other side of their face and their jaw twisted up in this grimace and they could no longer see straight and had to hide on the bottom.

Hm, my mother said.

Oh, sorry, Steve said.

No, I think it's great you're talking about puberty to my twelve-year-old daughter, ha.

Sorry.

It's fine. As long as it's about fish, she's fine.

I don't see what the big deal is, I said.

That's exactly right, my mother said. And we hope to keep that going another year or two.

What about you, Sheri, Steve said to my mother. What's your favorite fish?

I never get to go into the aquarium. I just pick her up. Being a parent is a lot like running a service: taxi, laundry, cooking, cleaning, tutoring, counseling, excursions.

You must have a favorite, though?

I don't have time for favorites. I work, I take care of Caitlin, and that's it.

Sorry, I said.

No. No. God, you must both think I'm awful right now, that I'm a terrible mother. I love you, sweet pea, and I love everything we do together. I'm just saying there's not time to focus on anything else.

Steve had his napkin up, in both hands, as if he were going to wipe his mouth, but he wasn't moving.

Sorry, my mother said. You must be wondering why you're seeing me.

Well, you're hot. That's one reason. Steve did his chuckle bounce, and my mother smiled despite herself. And you can wrestle containers and cranes, so that's useful. In case I'm ever in a situation where containers are coming after me.

My mother gave one of his biceps a love punch.

But what's your favorite fish? I asked.

Maybe from childhood, Steve suggested.

She never talks about that, I said.

Oh.

Wow, my mother said. There's no limit to how far I can sink during this dinner. Okay, one fish. I must be able to think of a fish. I'm thinking of the supermarket, the fish section, but I'm guessing you want something not on ice or wrapped in plastic.

Steve laughed. He was the nicest man she had ever brought home. Looking back, I can see he was delighted by her right from the beginning, genuinely delighted.

Okay. We lived in a shitty place. A shack on the highway, water dripping through the ceiling. I'm not going to say more. But next door, sharing the same dirt, we had a family from Japan. Asians are supposed to be rich, but these ones weren't. I don't know what went wrong. But the man dug a pit, and we thought he was going to roast a pig. We thought he might be Hawaiian. But he lined it with plastic and rocks and some plants and made a pond, and had four koi carps in there.

That sounds nice, Steve said.

A pearl in a toilet, my mother said. One of the koi was orange and white, the colors swirled together, and I named her Angel. And the man put an old wooden chair beside the pond so that I could sit. He never used it. He always stood. But he left this chair for me. I never even spoke to him, or thanked him. I feel so bad about it now. We were really racist back then. This was the early seventies, when I was about your age. But he gave me a place to escape to. I'd always sit out there, usually in the rain, and watch Angel gliding around her tiny pond as if she owned the palace ponds. And I liked that the rain never touched her.

I could see the drops on the surface. She'd tilt up to grab food, but otherwise she was hovering just below, safe and removed from everything.

Steve and I didn't say anything. We all sat in silence, my mother looking down at the table, lost in another time, and I remember thinking she was just like me, as if I had lived already, more than twenty years earlier.

Steve spent the night. I could hear their breathing, and small cries from my mother as if she were hurt, but I knew to stay in my room and keep quiet. My mother had explained many times that some parts of her life were hers. I had my three pillows, my pillow palace, a kind of nest or cave, and I sank away there.

In the morning, Steve made cinnamon toast, which was something new. Butter and then sugar and cinnamon. He put one piece faceup on my plate and then cut another piece on its diagonals to make four triangles, and with these he made a pyramid.

Egyptian toast, he said. With cinnamon from the Nile. What fish are in the Nile?

The Pharaoh Fish, Steve said, and raised his eyebrows. He leaned in close and whispered so my mother wouldn't hear. They have scales of red marble, very heavy, and fins of gold.

There are no fish like that.

Have you been to the Nile?

No.

Well I used to live there, at the bottom of the river. Don't tell your mother. The Pharaoh Fish gathered all along the bottom as if they were a garden of gold. They had big lips but never opened their mouths. They were very quiet. But they were keeping all the gold for the next pharaoh.

How come I haven't heard about the Pharaoh Fish?

Well you have now, and you have to keep it a secret because of the gold. Five thousand years ago, someone told, and the biggest fish had to leave the river and burrow through sand and try to hide. The Great Pyramids are their fins sticking up out of the sand. They were the biggest Pharaoh Fish.

I laughed and punched his arm the way my mother did. No fish are that big, I said. The largest fish is the whale shark.

Now, he said. But not back then.

I was distracted all morning at school thinking about the Pharaoh Fish. I knew Steve was making them up, but I loved the idea of their golden fins and red marble scales, and I could see them all waiting at the bottom of the river, their bellies on sand.

Shalini, I said. We have to make a Pharaoh Fish.

We had just begun art period, and Shalini already had strips of newspaper ready for Lakshmi Rudolph's legs.

What is a Pharaoh Fish?

They have red scales and golden fins.

I've seen golden fish. But I think they're Buddhist.

Where have you seen them?

On tiles on walls in India, I think. And you can buy plastic ones, or as balloons.

Do people pray to them?

I guess so.

That's my religion then. I'm Buddhist.

Shalini laughed. You can't just be a new religion.

There were two ways to make shapes for paper-mache, using wire or balloons, and we had some long skinny balloons, so I blew up one of these and began wrapping it in Shalini's strips. I imagined great temples with fish altars, and I would become a priestess. I would wear red makeup, with golden lips and eyebrows.

What's this, Caitlin? Mr. Gustafson asked. He looked out of breath from running around the room. His nostrils working hard.

A golden fish. It will have red scales and golden fins.

Let's keep focused on task. We want Rudolph to have legs, right, so he can lead the sleigh?

But the golden fish is for my religion. I'm Buddhist.

You're Buddhist?

Yes.

Caitlin.

I am.

What will your mother have to say about that?

She'll say I'm Buddhist. I'm a vegetarian, and I pray to the golden fish, and I may become a priestess.

Caitlin. You eat the school lunch. I know you're not Buddhist. And don't we already have enough religions? We need a few people to still be Christian.

I pray to the golden fish. This is my god.

Okay, fine. Pray to the fish. I'm going to make a papermache of my butt and pray to that.

Mr. Gustafson left then to try to save the sleigh. He had four kids working, but it looked like a fence with scraps blown against it, like something at the dump.

You're in trouble, Shalini whispered in my ear, leaning close. She was deliriously happy about it. All the little hairs stood up on my neck and I had goose bumps. Shalini could make me shiver, as if my entire body were a bell that had just been struck.

In the aquarium, I found the old man looking at a grumpy silver ghost.

Bright face in a grimace, squared head, and fins of transparent lace. Every movement a performance, fairy flight. I had watched him before, and I was always afraid the other fish would eat his fins. I think that's why he looked so unhappy. He couldn't fit anywhere to hide. Always drifting around in the open sections.

He's from the Mediterranean, the old man said. Very fancy. Some sort of royalty.

Maybe that's why he's unhappy.

I've never believed the rich are unhappy. I think they close their doors on us and then can't stop laughing.

Have you seen the photo? I asked.

Yes.

Almost as big as the diver. I can't imagine this small fish becoming that. And standing straight up and down in the water. I still don't see how it isn't just eaten right away.

The poor never get it together, the old man said. They feed on each other. It would be so easy to kill all the rich. There are so few of them. But we never do it.

Killing?

Sorry. I would never hurt anybody, of course. But does it seem fair to be poor?

No.

Well then. I'm okay if someone nibbles this guy's fins a bit. He looks like a boss, that square shiny face, that mouth. He's called the dealfish, even, and isn't that what bosses do, make deals using other people's lives?

The old man turned away from the tank then and walked across the aisle to where trout hung in some invisible current, all facing the same way, swimming to nowhere.

Hard to get excited about freshwater fish, he said. They're just like us, nothing exotic. Some sticks and rocks, cold, bundled up in a group, shivering. We're looking at the good people of Seattle right here.

I wish people looked like this, I said.

Ha. You're right. It would be an improvement.

The trout eyes looked alarmed, always, as if any sudden movement could make them bolt. Mouths about to say something, just starting to open.

I wish they could speak, I said.

What would they say?

I studied the trout. Come back, I finally said. Join us. Watch out.

The old man chuckled. Water's cold, he said in a trout voice. Can someone turn up the heater? And how about throwing a can of corn in here?

And some bread, I said. Cinnamon toast. My mother has a new boyfriend, named Steve. He made me cinnamon toast this morning.

Does your mother have a lot of boyfriends?

Some.

And what's she like with her boyfriends?

I don't know.

Is she happy?

I guess.

Hm. I hope she's happy.

I didn't like talking about my mother with the old man. He had never even met her. I walked away toward the river otters. They always cheered me up. I leaned my forehead against the cold glass and watched them run and slide into each other.

Not a care in the world, he said. He had followed me. They live only to play.

Dark slick bodies so smooth and fast, twisting around each other, leaping out of the water and running on their fins. They were like nothing else. The penguins were close, maybe, but not really. I wanted to be a river otter even more than I wanted to be the ghost pipefish. Making new clusters of stars was no good if you ended up alone.

Overtime, my mother said when I got in the car.

Okay, I said, but I wasn't happy. I wanted to go home to have dinner and sleep. We woke up at five every morning to leave by six, because my mother had to start work by seven.

We drove down Alaskan Way in the rain and then crossed over Harbor Island and the West Seattle Bridge onto West Marginal Way Southwest. Land of the container. Stacks of them everywhere, red and blue and white.

Colors of the flag, I said.

What?

I just realized, the containers are all the colors of the flag. And the ships are red or blue on their hulls, and white above, and the cranes are red.

You're right, my mother said. I never noticed that. Good eye. Black on the sides of the hulls, and some green and gray mixed into the containers, but yeah, mostly it's all one big flag. Your mother is Betsy Ross.

It was getting dark as we pulled in, headlights on, the air streaked. Big floodlights higher up, all the sky lit and falling. My favorite kind of rain.

It'll be a late one, my mother said. Midnight. So here's ten dollars for the food truck, when you get hungry. I'll come see you on my break, at about nine, no later than ten.

My mother had several smudges of oil on her cheeks. Her ponytail flattened from her helmet. Be good and don't wander off. She kissed me then and grabbed her helmet and jogged away across the pavement.

Overtime was two or three times a week, but we never knew when. My mother always said yes, because this was our way to get ahead. Pay and a half, which meant almost fifteen dollars an hour.

I sat in the car awhile, listening to the ticking of the engine as it cooled and pinpricks of rain on the roof. The bench seat going cold, windows fogging. Flashing yellow lights on the smaller cranes as they found each container a home, red lights high on the cranes that reached over the water and unloaded ships. White light for each small box that held a person. My mother one of the darker shadow figures on the ground, without light.

I always wondered what was inside the containers. From all over the world, holding anything. Customs officers in their new Jeeps always here, checking, opening steel doors and shining flashlights.

The car too cold, so I stepped carefully through puddles to the ramp that led up to the lounge. Wheelchair access, but why would anyone in a wheelchair come here? A portable office with fluorescent lights, thin gray carpet, and bare walls. Plastic chairs, several bulletin boards, and three customs officers stirring cups of coffee in a corner, talking quietly.

At the other end, a small office where a secretary sat during the day, but no one at night. I knew them all from school holidays, when I spent a lot of time here. Darla, who liked my drawings and always talked with me, Liz, who didn't like kids, Mary, who listened to music and could never hear me, and several others. There were other portable offices next to this one, and everyone kept moving around, carrying papers and coffee mugs and rain jackets.

I settled in for the long wait. I had my homework, which wasn't much, but I unzipped my backpack and pulled out the math book. Fractions and percentages. Mr. Gustafson had taught us to tell stories from our own lives for each problem. If ten people made a family, and my mother and I were the only two, we were one-fifth of a family. If a shark swam into a school of forty fish and ate 10 percent, there were four less fish.

Do you have a parent here, or guardian?

It was one of the customs officers. He was staring down at me, holding his coffee. Short hair, older. A gun on his hip.

Leave her alone, Bill, one of the others said.

How old are you?

I'm twelve, I said. I was afraid of this man. He wanted to hurt someone. That was clear.

Where is your parent or guardian?

My mother is working overtime.

Single mother?

Bill. Cut it out.

Bill ignored them, kept staring down at me. What's her name?

Sheri Thompson.

Sheri Thompson. You tell her to come see me. Inspector Bigby.

I couldn't move. He was like a dog, watching and ready to bite. Skin reddish, weathered, shaven but all the dark holes of his whiskers visible. Then he turned away and the others laughed and they walked out.

This portable like its own tank, lit from above, but at the aquarium, they were careful which fish went together. They would never have let Bill in. Real life was more like the ocean, where any predator might come along at any time.

I couldn't do my homework. I couldn't focus. I put away the math book and just sat there alone for hours, afraid to move, listening to the rain on the roof and the diesel engines of the cranes. I was afraid Bill would come back, afraid also that he was out there looking for my mother. I didn't know what he'd do if he found her. I didn't know whether we were in trouble.

When my mother finally arrived, I ran to her.

She picked me up, something she never did anymore.

What happened? she asked. What's wrong?

I tried to answer, but I was crying against her neck, these awful out-of-control sobs.

She set me down. Caitlin, you have to tell me, right now.

Inspector Bigby, I said. He asked if I had a parent, and he wants to see you. He's one of the customs officers.

My mother looked out the window, as if he might be watching us right now.

His first name is Bill, and he's mean, and they were laughing.

Come with me right now, she said. We're going to the car. Walk fast.

I grabbed my backpack and we hurried through the rain, exposed for anyone to see. Big floodlights.

I jumped in and my mother held the door. I have to tell my foreman I'm leaving, she said. I'll be right back.

Don't go, I said. I told him your name.

It's okay, Caitlin. It's going to be okay.

My mother jogged away then through the rain, still wearing her helmet. I was afraid she wouldn't come back. Bill would take her in his new Jeep to some prison even though she hadn't done anything wrong, and I would never see her again. Locked away somewhere.

And she was gone a long time. Needles of rain on the roof of the car, bright lights in a darkness swallowing my mother.

But she did return, and we drove slowly through the yard, to the gate where she stopped and gave her ID, and then we were free, back on West Marginal Way Southwest and then the bridge.

When we arrived home, my mother parked in front of

our apartment, turned off the engine, and slumped forward against the wheel.

I'm sorry, I said.

No, sweet pea, she said, quiet now. It's not your fault. And it will never happen again. I think there's some law that says I can't leave you alone, without an adult. So I won't do overtime. We should still be okay. I'll have enough for rent, and food and gas, and you have your aquarium pass. I can afford the water and heat. We just won't have any extras. I'll cancel the phone and TV, if I can.

Will we still get ahead?

My mother laughed. Sweet pea. You've been listening to me too much. It'll be okay. I won't be putting anything into retirement for me or college for you. That's what I meant by getting ahead. Maybe saving for a house, but that wasn't happening anyway. But you can still go to college. You just have to study hard, okay?

During art period, I made a paper-mache of Inspector Bigby. I didn't use a balloon, because I was going to be sticking him with a lot of needles. I wadded up newspaper and then wrapped it in wet strips. I would paint his head red and uniform white.

And what is this? Mr. Gustafson asked.

Inspector Bigby.

Is he part of the Buddhist pantheon?

What?

Is he one of your Buddhist gods, like the golden fish? Will he be riding in the sleigh?

No.

Well then?

I ripped Inspector Bigby into pieces, tore at the newspaper and let it fall to the floor. Then I started crying. I couldn't help it.

Great, Mr. Gustafson said. Just what I need. Shalini, can you take Caitlin to the bathroom to cry?

Everyone was looking at me. I kept my head down as Shalini led me out by the hand. I could see her golden bracelets, hoops that slid and bounced, and we escaped down the hallway to the bathrooms.

We were twelve years old. She didn't have any wise words for me, or even tell me things would be okay. I wasn't able to tell her what was wrong. But I remember standing in front of the mirror, my eyes red, and she hugged me from behind. Pressed all against my back, arms pulling tight, her face tucked in close against my neck, feel of her breath. Her hair so black against my blond in the mirror. It's the clearest image I have of us, because of that stupid mirror, and my face crumpling in self-pity, like any kid seeing herself cry.

The old man knew right away. What's wrong? he asked.

I had found him resting on a bench near the jellyfish. I sat down and leaned against him and he put his arm around me.

It's all right, he said.

Cold smell of his coat. He must have just arrived. Very few people here today, dark corridors warm and humid and private. Crowded in the summer, but who would go to an aquarium in December?

Did you know the jellyfish aren't fish? I asked.

That makes sense, the old man said. I guess I didn't really know, though.

And they've lived for five hundred million or maybe even seven hundred million years. They're older than anything.

I hid against the old man and watched the jellyfish rise and fall. Slow pulse of life, made of nothing, from another world.

I can't imagine seven hundred million years, he finally said. It doesn't mean anything to me. Four or five times as old as dinosaurs, but who can look back before dinosaurs, before sharks? It's the same as trying to imagine, well, I don't know what. South America would be part of Africa then, I think, or who knows, and no birds. Can you imagine no birds? And nothing yet learned to crawl. I guess there were plants, but what kind of plants? Were there even plants? Maybe a few ferns?

There were no plants, I said. No plants on land.

Holy smokes.

I wish we had a box jellyfish, I said.

Why's that?

They have twenty-four eyes and four brains, and two of the eyes might be able to see.

What do you mean? Don't all eyes see?

They only sense light, jellyfish eyes. But the box jellyfish might be able to see. A jellyfish might have been the first thing to ever see.

Where do you learn this stuff?

Fish Mike.

What's that?

He gives a talk here, every two weeks. The last one was about jellyfish.

What else did he say?

That a hundred years from now, most of the fish might be gone, and we might be back to only jellyfish. He said we should enjoy the fish now, because this is a last look.

I still can't believe there were no plants, the old man said. I'm imagining a world of only rock and sea, nothing else, just rock and sea, and the only thing living in the sea are jellyfish. They have the entire planet to themselves. And now I hear they're getting it back, as if time is reversing. You're only twelve years old, but do you know that what you've said today is more amazing than anything I've heard in my entire life?

I sat up and looked at the old man. I thought he was making fun of me, but he wasn't laughing. He seemed serious. He put his hand on my head, the way my mother sometimes did.

Caitlin, he said. I feel so lucky to be here with you.

I knew something was wrong. Even at age twelve, I knew you don't just meet an old man like this. But I needed him, so I ignored anything that seemed creepy. I settled in against him again, his arm around me, and I looked at the jellyfish in their slow and endless pulsing, heartbeat before there was any such thing as a heart, and I felt my life become possible. The old man had said I was amazing, and in that moment, I felt I might become anything.

So what's wrong? the old man asked. Why are you upset today? You can tell me.

I didn't know how to speak about Inspector Bigby. He wasn't just a man. He was part of some larger threat, my mother taken away from me, and I didn't know if we had done anything wrong. I was just afraid, but I was afraid of everything.

I'm sorry, he said. Caitlin. You're breathing really quickly right now. Are you okay? Are you having some kind of panic attack?

I couldn't answer.

Caitlin. You have to calm down.

He put his hand on my chest.

God, your heart is racing. Please say something.

The old man let go of me and stood up. I've never been good at this, he said. I'm sorry, I have to go. He left then, walking very fast for an old man, running away, and it seemed like he was rising uphill, the floor tilting, and I was sliding downward.

Please, I said, but my voice was so quiet. I was alone in this dark thin hallway, fallen to the bottom, and I curled on the bench and watched the jellyfish above. Rings of light, moons come alive. My heart felt made of rock, dark and hard, but the jellyfish were made of something calmer, reassuring. Slow drift endless, begun so long ago. They were beautiful, and if you looked at them long enough, you could believe they were made only for beauty.

We know so much more now about ocean acidification, and I should hate the jellyfish as a sign of all that we've destroyed. In my lifetime, the reefs will melt away, dissolved. By the end of the century, nearly all fish will be gone. The entire legacy of humanity will be only one thing, a line of red goop in the paleo-oceanographic record, a time of no calcium carbonate shells that will stretch on for several million years. The sadness of our stupidity is overwhelming. But when I watch a moon jelly, its umbrella constellation pulsing into endless night, I think perhaps it's all okay.

My mother was able to live without a future. This was perhaps her best quality, that she never despaired. And she knew when to cheer me up. That evening, instead of driving home, we went for pizza and a movie, and it wasn't a date with Steve. I had my mother all to myself.

The pizza had artichoke hearts, like jellyfish gone opaque and yellowed, washed up on a beach of dough.

I watched the jellyfish today, I told my mother.

How are things going for them? Any big changes?

Mom.

My mother was smiling. Have they noticed yet that they're in a tank?

They might have been the first things to see. Ever.

What do you mean?

I mean nothing else could see. There was this whole world, and nothing could see it.

That is cool, I have to admit. You're a trip, Caitlin. I never thought of that, the planet before anything could see it. There might as well have been no day, no light.

Yeah.

And then the jellyfish opened their eyes.

Yeah.

I imagine them like dogs sleeping on a carpet, slouched down and then one of them puts its head up and takes a look.

Mom.

Sorry. I'm not a fishhead like you. I don't see the world as fish. I see dogs.

Can we get a dog?

Caitlin. You know you're allergic.

I want one anyway.

That's my daughter. I'm just like you. I've always wanted the things I can't have. But the trick is to just focus on the pizza and enjoy the salt and cheese. And then we watch a movie, and then we go to sleep. Close your eyes now and enjoy the salt and fat.

I tried it. I closed my eyes and focused on salt and fat and oil, and it was good. I was only a mouth in the darkness.

I watched only a few parts of the movie. Mostly I watched the shifting light on the balconies above us, great rock formations on a seawall extending upward to a surface I couldn't see. We were set back in the lowest cave, the safest place, in the largest school, all hung vertical like razorfish but not inverted. The roof above us the floor to another cave. All eyes peering outward into endless expanse, open ocean, heavy curtains on the walls in folds like dark rippling of light in the depths, always seeming to move closer. The faces around me all registering the same emotions at once and maintaining perfect spacing, flash of cheeks as they turned their heads and then gone in darkness again. Crunching sounds as they fed on the reef, always feeding even as they watched.

All was the same as when I watched TV with my mother at home, except now we were in a large school. Two of us or two hundred of us, there was no difference. All silent still, watching, looking outward into the light, waiting. And the sea itself unchanged. Sound magnified, booming, and only sound marked time.

Even as a kid, I felt this sense that there was no why to any fish or person. The school could be one hundred and ninety-nine instead of two hundred, and this would have no effect on the ocean, no effect on sound or time or light. I was always vanishing. In that theater, I appeared and disappeared and reappeared, all without effect, and the rock above remained constant, and the formless air. I tried to do what my mother did, tasting the salt and fat and oil and now watching patterns of light before sleep, but I could never immerse. I was never able to find my way into any tank at all.

We drove home in darkness, this car the smallest cave, glow of instrument lights on my mother's face. Moving at impossible speed, as if our wheels had no contact with ground. My mother lost in the movie still. She had grabbed my hand in the tense or sad moments. I don't think she was even aware she did it. Immersion came naturally to her.

When we arrived home, she was tired and quiet and we simply went to bed. She didn't make me go to my own room, but her bed might as well have stretched hundreds of feet across. The freedom of pizza and a movie was over. Now there was only her exhaustion and another day of hard work waiting after a sleep too short.

Too soon we were back in the car, driving again in darkness, north in a stream of lights, some massive current sweeping all of us toward the greater light. Seattle something resting on the ocean floor, enormous starfish with bright ridges and fingers of black between. Bioluminescent glow pulling everything near, individual lights of aircraft in the depths above like deep-sea anglers. Their bodies invisible, shapes drifting through darkness and cold and no sound. Nothing known.

I could believe the day would never come. Daylight seemed unlikely, and unwanted. The city so much more beautiful in darkness. I was bundled in my jacket and hood against the cold, and I would have drifted along with my mother for any length of time without end, but she left me at the curb of Gatzert Elementary, saying have a good day, sweet pea, giving me a kiss that barely touched my cheek. Her breath still heavy, still half asleep, each exhale a kind of sigh. And then she was gone, and I walked to the front doors where the janitor always let me in. In another hour, teachers would arrive, and during the half hour after that, the other kids. But I was always the first except the janitor, who seemed to live here through the night.

I waited on the only bench, outside the principal's office. All chairs were kept inside rooms, leaving the hallways smooth and clear, long tubes to direct the surge of each tide of students and teachers. The rooms rock pools, microcosms, left stagnant and then swept away again. A world with many moons, most of them invisible, the janitor and I the only riders at six thirty and nowhere to cling.

At seven thirty, the next low tide, he unlocked the rooms, let each door swing free, and each room begin to fill with the returning sea, teachers brought in slowly by the current, sleepwalkers with papers and books and mugs of coffee, jackets dripping from the rain outside, every floor becoming a slick.

I think most fish would not survive so many moons and tides. I think the current would exhaust them, and they'd become confused. The surge would pull them away from whatever anemone or rock or bit of sand or coral was home, and in all the cycles afterward they'd lose direction and never find their way back. What we've become is very strange.

At twelve, I had only the sense of pressure, some premonition, riding each surge and waiting for the counterpull, believing, perhaps, that all would release at some point. Each day was longer than the days now, and my own end not yet possible. It was a simpler mind, more direct and responsive. We live through evolution ourselves, each of us, progressing through different apprehensions of the world, at each age forgetting the last age, every previous mind erased. We no longer see the same world at all.

So perhaps I'm wrong about immersion. Not sensing the tank doesn't mean it's not there, and even loneliness must be in some way contained. The teachers nodded to me as they passed, mumbled hello, but I had sat there so many mornings I had become like rock or coral, no more than structure.

Shalini was the one I waited for. She always arrived sleepy with her backpack and Tupperware, sat down on the bench and collapsed against me. I'm so tired, she said. She could fall asleep in a car, so I was catching her only minutes from dreams.

I've been awake for three hours, I said.

Shh, she said. I'm sleeping. She had her arms around me and I closed my eyes but then the bell rang, as it always did, and we rose and she clung to my arm. My mother said you can come over tomorrow for a sleepover, she said.

Yay!

Shh.

Hello clump of Shalini-Caitlin, Mr. Gustafson said. Perhaps you can be two people today?

Shalini always ignored him, but we did have to separate to fit into two seats. I was so happy about the sleepover, I couldn't stop smiling, even through fractions and percentages. Having something to look forward to changes everything. I've always needed a future. I can't live without one.

I didn't know whether I would find the old man. As I approached the aquarium, I slowed down, despite the rain, because I was afraid I'd never see him again. The aquarium would be far too lonely now without him. Pier 59 only a building projecting out into the sea, another drab shape in the gray. The rain very cold, close to becoming snow. Day without light, the air hung in dark sheets and columns that swept in over the water.

He was waiting in the first corridor, sitting slumped in a dark blue sweater, his hair rising up in thin fans, wild faint sprays from having worn a hat. Dark form of him otherwise camouflaged, head speckled.

Caitlin, he said, and rose. I'm very sorry. Will you forgive an old man for his weakness?

Hi, I said.

Hi. What fish would you like to see today?

Um. I looked around, worlds within worlds all within reach. I was so happy he was still here, that he hadn't left forever. The razorfish, I said. I was thinking of the razorfish yesterday, at the movie theater. I went to a movie with my mom.

What movie?

I don't know.

You don't know?

I wasn't watching it.

Oh.

We walked then to a large tank of coral and tropical fish. The razorfish hung like tinsel, as if they knew Christmas was coming and wanted to help.

Poor buggers, the old man said. They think that's normal. And how do they get anywhere? If they swam forward, they'd stick in the bottom.

I've only seen them hang like that.

Well they're going to have to come up with something more.

My mother isn't doing overtime.

No? She was doing overtime?

Yeah.

Why?

So we could get ahead.

Hm.

But Inspector Bigby wanted to know where my parent or guardian was.

Inspector Bigby.

Yeah. I was afraid of him.

So that's why you were upset.

Yeah.

I'm sorry, Caitlin. I should have helped you more. And your mother's all alone, no family. I think I could try to help. I think I could do that. I had a long night. I'd like to stop being of no use to anyone. Do you think I could meet your mother? Do you think you could tell her about me?

The old man looked desperate, pleading with me. It was very strange. I knew something was wrong, but I didn't understand the possibilities. So I agreed. Okay, I said. Today?

No. The old man looked worried. He ran his hand through his hair, flattening the ruff. Maybe Monday. Let's do Monday. You can have the weekend to talk with her. Tell her all that we've done, looking at all the fish, all we've talked about. Have you told her anything about me?

No.

Nothing, huh? Well, that's too bad. That's very fast. But Monday. We'll do Monday.

She'll be here today.

No. Please. Let's wait a bit. And we can stop talking about this. Let's just walk around the aquarium. Have you seen the leafy seadragon?

Yeah. Of course. Everyone has seen the leafy seadragon.

Well, okay, but let's go look at him again.

The old man took my hand and we walked to the sea-dragon tank. Sand light blue, hairy green plants, and a sea horse become a golden branch, sprouting leaves that might have been wings. If you looked at her long enough, you could imagine trees coming alive, entire forests waking up and drifting across the land, speaking in whispers. No trunk vertical but all gone horizontal, moving along on their branches, roots hung in the air. I wanted to live in that world.

I've been watching this fish every day now, the old man said. A fish that lives only to hide. The other fish are hiding, too, but this one has gone too far. He's become unrecognizable, all twisted up like a branch, barely able to swim, fins useless. There has to be more than just hiding.

The old man sounded bitter. I'm disgusted by this fish, he said.

I looked at those bars of gold that somehow had become a body, and I couldn't imagine a more beautiful fish, even the ghost pipefish. What if a tree could grow into the shape of a salmon, or a field of grass grow like trout, mouths gasping toward the sun? Even now, I still believe metamorphosis is the greatest beauty. Snakes have adapted their coloring, birds their beaks and legs, and even a mountain goat can vanish with white hair, but only fish and insects can take another form. A praying mantis to match this seadragon, but so much less ornate. Fish can become corollary to anything, unlimited, not held to any base, able to transform beyond imagination. We're still finding new shapes in the ocean.

I'm not going to be this fish, the old man said. I refuse.

How could you be this fish?

Stunted as a person, kinked like that, choked, cowardly, hiding, always disappearing, like when I ran away yesterday.

The old man faced me then, got down on his knees, which looked painful. He took my hands in his. Damp cool skin, rough. Look, he said. You're just starting out. You have a long life ahead. I have only a little bit left. Other men are going to get down on their knees for you, offering you their lives, but what I'm offering is more. The end of a life is more, and my reasons are more pure. I love you more than any other man ever will.

I tried to pull my hands away, but he held on.

It's going to be tough times. Confusing for you. You won't be happy. But just remember that I love you and that I'll do anything for you now.

I was afraid of him. He wouldn't let go of my hands.

Please, he said. No. Don't misunderstand. Just tell your mother about me, and I'll meet her on Monday. Okay?

I nodded. My heart going so fast I thought it would never slow down again.

Okay, he said. You're the best little girl in the world, Caitlin. He let go then, and I turned and ran away down those dark corridors rimmed in light, all the fish watching, and didn't stop until I was in the lobby. I sat on a bench by the door, out of breath, and I wanted my mother to rescue me. It wasn't time yet, and I was afraid the old man would come out here. I had nowhere to hide, and it was too cold outside, icy rain a roar against all other sound.

The old man remained submerged with the fish, hidden away, and my mother finally appeared. I ran to her through the rain and wind and swung that heavy door and was safe.

Hey sweet pea. You're turning into a track star.

I didn't say anything in response. I didn't know where to start.

What's wrong?

I was looking down at my jeans, wet below the rim of my coat.

Caitlin, you have to tell me now.

Shalini invited me for a sleepover tomorrow. Can I go?

My mother laughed. Is that it? I thought something was wrong. Of course you can go.

She pulled away from the curb then and we drove through the flood, sprays of water rising on both sides, each car with fins like the dealfish, transparent, revealed in headlights. Day but dark, the seas drained, and all of us splashing along the bottom looking for another sea. Others passed, racing ahead, all drawn the same way. The most frantic flight.

I have her parents' phone number on the class list, my mother said. We'll call when we get home. And is it okay if Steve comes over for dinner?

Steve was already at our apartment when we arrived. We could hear his harmonica as we rose up the stairs, low sad song, Summertime. My mother stopped on the stairs and closed her eyes and we just listened for a while in the cold. A song that kept falling. When he was finished, he said I know you're there.

My mother smiled and we rose the rest the way. He was sitting against our door, legs stretched out and boots crossed, flowers on his lap and two bags of groceries beside him.

I thought I'd fix dinner, he said. Mexican night. Halibut fajitas, guacamole, margaritas. Un poco de salsa.

He rose and my mother gave him a squeeze and a kiss. Then we went in and they ignored me. While he worked in the kitchen, my mother pressed up against the back of him like a shell. I sat on the couch and did my homework, reading about kids who were building a tree fort together in some sunnier place.

Don't forget to call, I said.

My mother and Steve both looked up from some dream, startled to hear another voice.

Sorry, sweet pea, my mother said. I forgot. She detached from Steve and went to the wall for the phone. She looked up the number and dialed and I listened. They were inviting me early, just after lunch, to spend the whole day and then the night. I was so happy I started hopping up and down.

Look at you, Steve said. A Mexican jumping bean.

My mother hung up and said, Okay, after lunch tomorrow. Shalini's excited too. Don't hop, though. We'll get in trouble with the neighbors.

She went back to Steve, but I didn't care. I would have Shalini all to myself for almost a full day. I couldn't focus on the reading. I just sat on the couch and felt happy.

My mother and Steve were drinking margaritas in our big plastic water glasses, pink and blue, my mother getting louder from the drink, laughing and punching Steve and climbing all over him.

When dinner was ready, she sat close to him at our small round breakfast table and I was on the other side of the circle. A large plate of fajitas between us, thin strips of halibut and bell peppers, mushrooms and onions. Corn tortillas warmed up. A bowl of guacamole, jar of salsa. I took a big scoop of guacamole and a tortilla and started eating. I was starving.

Steve was doing his bouncing chuckle, and my mother was grabbing at his chest and stomach and arms, those biceps. But at one point he noticed me.

Hey, you're not having any fajitas, he said.

I don't eat fish, I said.

He looked so sad suddenly. It was immediate.

I'm sorry, he said. I should have known. And I told you this was my favorite fish, didn't I. The halibut. Those eyes.

It's okay, my mother said. She doesn't mind if we eat fish. It's a great dinner, and you'll be rewarded.

I'm sorry, Caitlin, he said.

It's okay.

My mother kissed him then and took him away again. They never resurfaced. Somehow we ate the rest of the dinner and he did dishes and we had ice cream for dessert and they went to bed and all of it happened without my becoming visible. I was in my room reading and fell asleep without knowing.

When I look back, I'm happy for my mother, and I think it's good she knew how to make me disappear. I think it was necessary, and I don't think I even felt bad at the time. Maybe a little lonely, but that was all. We were still in the same house together, and safe.

Shalini was waiting for me at her front door. Her mother behind her with painted eyes and a red dot on her forehead.

I shrieked, and Shalini shrieked, and we ran toward each other and collided and swung around in a circle, jumping up and down. Our mothers were laughing.

Shalini had a beautiful red and gold dress and hoops of gold on her arms, bare in the cold.

Come in, her mother was saying. Shalini, bring your friend inside.

Inside their house was like a palace. Not much bigger than our apartment, but no wall was bare. Thin veils hung like curtains, golden elephants on red carpets, candles and bright pillows and carved dark wood.

We took off our shoes and my mother drifted away and I hardly noticed. Smell of spices thick in the air, all that I smelled each day on Shalini at school but stronger now. Looking back, I'd guess it was clove and cardamom, turmeric and raisins, maybe even something sweeter, cinnamon or something else, but at the time, it was only a kind of magic, overwhelming. I had entered a new land entirely. This is what I've always loved about a city, all the worlds hidden away inside, largest of aquariums.

Shalini's father wore a business shirt and slacks, even on a Saturday. He shook my hand, and I think he had greeted my mother before she left, and then he disappeared too. He smelled like sweet smoke.

Shalini led me to her room down a narrow hallway. Stuffed animals and pillows covering her entire bed and much of the floor, a goddess with golden arms on her wall. At least twenty arms like Shalini's, each holding a red flower against black velvet, as if a person might take any form, as varied as fish and as brightly colored.

I wish you had that many arms, I told Shalini.

How would I ever put on a shirt?

I laughed and pulled her onto the bed. A soft comforter and all the pillows, much softer than my bed. I had my nose in her hair, smelling her, and I put my hands inside her shirt, feeling her skin. Here are two extra arms, I said. I could feel goose bumps all along my arms and down my back. Her stomach smooth and warm, heart and breath fast. We can be like fish, I said. Let's get under the covers.

So we threw the pillows and stuffed animals off the bed, got under the comforter, and I pulled it over our heads. We're a thousand feet down, I said. There's no light. And no sound.

Shalini giggled.

Shh, I said. We can't hear anything.

Shalini put her mouth on my ear and breathed, slow weight of the ocean and my spine curling like a shrimp. She held my head in both hands and kept her mouth to my ear and I was arched against her, pressing hard, caught in place, almost paralyzed.

You're my fish, she whispered. I've caught you.

She put her leg over me, and now I was being pressed down, held down against the bottom of the ocean, and this was exactly what I wanted. She pulled off my shirt and lifted her dress until we were skin against skin and I could breathe her in and she climbed onto my back and bit my neck and I moaned and this was my first pleasure, my first memory of pleasure.

We were twelve, and we of course knew nothing, but this was the day of my second birth. Shalini pulled off all my clothes and wore only her bracelets and we moved in darkness guided by feel, without idea, the purest desire, and I wish I could return to that first moment, our own Eden, innocence and desire the same.

By the time my mother picked me up the next morning, I was jangly from lack of sleep, buzzing inside. My spine alive as a sea horse fin, fluttering.

You look like a zombie, my mother said. A happy zombie. What did you do?

We swam, I said. Floated.

I didn't know they had a pool. It must be inside and heated? But their house is small.

Yes, I lied.

The drive was very strange, being in a car, seeing the

world outside pass by. All of it had changed. Bright and clear and small, even though there was no sun. The air without distance, the Space Needle as close as any house beside us. The way a fish can hang in stillness if the tank water is clear and calm enough. Suspended, held by nothing at all. Time no longer linked to object, the world muffled and without echo, without pressure, without movement.

I went to bed as soon as we arrived, slept through the afternoon until my mother woke me for dinner.

I don't know about sleepovers, my mother said. You do need to sleep. They're not called wakeovers. Shalini's parents did nothing to make you sleep?

I felt so heavy I couldn't answer. Lying in some deep-sea trench, all the weight above, unable to keep my eyes open.

I hope you can sleep tonight. We have to get you up and moving for a few hours at least.

My mother pulled me out of bed, made me walk and drink and eat and talk, all of which I observed from far away. All I could think of was Shalini. And then I remembered the old man.

Someone wants to meet you tomorrow, I said. At the aquarium. An old man.

An old man? Someone who works there?

No.

Well who then?

I was still submerged. I regretted trying to talk about this with her. Just someone.

Do you know him?

Yes.

How?

We talk about the fish. He's kind of like the three-spot frogfish. His hair and his old hands.

How long has this been going on?

I don't know.

You've been talking with some old man and you didn't tell me?

I closed my eyes and drifted back down, the pull irresistible.

Caitlin. My mother grabbed my chin and made me look up at her. I was sitting at the table and she was standing. What is his name?

I don't know.

Has he made any plans with you?

What?

Has he offered to take you anywhere?

I couldn't think. No, I said, and then I remembered. Just the Sea of Cortez, in Mexico, to see manta rays. They do backflips.

Caitlin! my mother yelled. That voice jolted me awake. Fear in both of us. You are not leaving school tomorrow, she said. You are going to stay right there. And I'll come as soon as I can, then we'll drive to the aquarium, and we'll arrive with the police.

No, I said. He's my friend.

Has he touched you?

What?

Has he touched you?

No. I mean I just sat with him and he hugged me. He was helping me.

Has he ever touched your chest?

No. I mean yeah, but just because I was panicking and my heart was going fast.

Caitlin! My mother slapped me, hard. How can you be so fucking stupid?

I was crying and running for my room, but my mother was pulling me back, grabbing at me. Sweet pea, she was saying. I'm sorry. Caitlin, I'm so sorry.

She tackled me in the hallway. She was crying. Caitlin, Caitlin, my baby. I'm sorry. But you can't do this to me.

I hadn't done anything. And I kept twisting, trying to get away from her, but she had clamped down tight and wasn't letting go.

Baby, she said. Did he say he loved you?

Yes.

My mother howled, some deep animal pain. Her entire body shaking as she cried. Her arm tight across my neck and her wet cheek against mine. I was so frightened. I didn't know what had happened.

I have to call the police, she said. I have to call right now, so they can be ready tomorrow.

Please don't, I said. But my mother left me on the floor and went to the kitchen to call. I went to my bed and hid under the comforter and felt so sorry for the old man. He was kind. He was only good. And tomorrow he'd be sitting there on the bench or looking at some fish in a tank and the police would come in and grab him and take him away and I'd never see him again. And there was no way to warn him.

I could hear my mother on the phone. He touched her. She's only twelve. He had plans to take her away to Mexico. He told her he loved her.

I slept that night only because I was exhausted, and I kept waking from dreams of panic, being chased, and that feeling remained in the day, the closest I've ever felt to doom. My hour-and-a-half wait at school in the fluorescent hallways was unbearable. Shalini arrived only a few minutes before class, and she was smiling but then saw my face.

What's wrong? she asked.

The police are coming. There's an old man I've been talking to, in the aquarium. He's my friend.

Shalini didn't understand, and what I saw then was

something new. The police taking me away from my mother, because she had left me alone with an old man, because she wasn't there. No parent or guardian.

I couldn't breathe. My heart yanking.

Caitlin! she said, and I woke up in the nurse's office, on a thin bed with my feet up on pillows. No Shalini. Only a nurse.

Where's my mother?

Shh, the nurse said. She was a big woman. You need to rest. You're okay. We've called your mother and she can't leave work right now. She'll be here this afternoon by two thirty.

The room cold and empty, sterile, a large window of gray, day without light. No clouds visible but only a deadening, no air, all come close.

The nurse left me, and I lay still for a very long time, cocooned, staring out that window into nothing. I wanted Shalini.

Then another woman came in. Hi Caitlin, she said. I'm Evelyn. I'm here just to say hello, to find out how you're feeling. You can talk with me.

She was watching my eyes, my mouth. She sat in a rolling office chair and scooted closer. How are you feeling?

I don't know.

Are you tired?

Yes.

Are you sad?

Yes.

What are you sad about?

Evelyn was staring at me as if I were in a tank, some new

species first swimming in the open to be observed. My arms become fins again, but not of lace or leaves. They felt heavy as rock, fins made of stone, unable to grab at the water. Stuck on the ocean floor, held down as eyes peered in, magnified.

Caitlin, you can talk to me. Are you worried about something?

She would take me away from my mother. I knew that. I knew she had the power to twist the world and change everything. I had to tell her nothing. I'm okay, I said.

You don't seem okay.

I just didn't feel like eating breakfast. I'm dizzy. I need some food.

Okay. Evelyn didn't believe me, I could tell. Your cheek seems a little bit puffy, she said. Did your mother hit you?

The police came in next. They weren't waiting for my mother. A man and a woman, then the man left. This woman wore a pistol and baton, a padded jacket. As if the old man or my mother were dangerous and might attack.

You are Caitlin Thompson?

I nodded.

Birthdate September 24, 1982?

Yes.

Mother Sheri Thompson, birthdate July 7, 1961?

Yes.

Please give a description of the man you've met at the Seattle Aquarium. The policewoman wasn't even looking at me. Focused on her notepad. She had a ponytail and was younger than my mother. She smelled like shoe polish and leather.

He's my friend.

What does he look like?

Like the three-spot frogfish.

Please describe how he looks.

He's not guarding eggs, but he has the same splotchy skin.

The woman lowered her pad and looked at me finally. Caitlin, she said. You have to help me here. I'm trying to protect you. Has this man touched you?

It was only hugs. Just being nice to me.

How often has he done this?

I don't know.

How often?

Maybe a couple times. He's my friend.

Has he touched your chest?

Just because I was afraid. I was panicking.

What were you panicking about?

I can't say.

You can't say?

No.

Caitlin, this man is in big trouble, and you are in big trouble. You need to tell me everything. I can stay here all day, and all tomorrow, and all of the next day and every day until you tell me everything. You cannot make me go away. Do you understand?

I hate you.

That's okay. You can hate me. But you're going to tell me everything. What were you panicking about?

I closed my eyes and tried to sink down into the deepest water, into darkness. My heart pumping fast, red flashes in my eyelids, but I would sink where she could not reach me, where no one could reach me.

Caitlin, she was saying again, but muffled and weak and far away, and she would not touch me. I knew that. They all cared so much about touching, they wouldn't dare. So I could close my eyes and sink away and there was nothing they could do. They'd never find out about Inspector Bigby or no parent or guardian or what the old man looked like or what had happened between us. If I could fall down far enough, I would be safe.

It was an eternity before my mother arrived. She was out of breath, had been running from the car. She still had her work clothes on, overalls and boots.

She saw the police, the counselor, the nurse. What are you all doing here?

We've been talking with your daughter, Evelyn said. We're concerned about what's happening at the aquarium and also at home.

I didn't tell them anything, I said.

What? My mother looked confused.

What is there to tell? Evelyn asked.

The police were moving in closer.

What are you talking about? my mother asked.

Have you struck your daughter?

Leave her alone! I yelled, and I ran to my mother, put my arms around her and couldn't help crying, these sobs that came in heaves.

There's a man at the aquarium, my mother said. He's been touching my daughter, making plans to take her away to Mexico, telling her he loves her. You all need to pull your heads out of your asses. We're going to the aquarium now to talk to this man.

He's my friend, I sobbed, but I could hardly make words. My mother was hugging me tight, rubbing my back.

Mrs. Thompson, you need to cooperate here, the policeman said. He had a low voice.

And you need to do your job. I'll talk about how you wouldn't do anything to protect a twelve-year-old girl and just let this man go free and now he could be wandering around anywhere in the city looking for someone else's daughter. And it's not missus. Just Thompson.

No one said anything for a while after that. I didn't dare look at them. I held on to my mother and kept my eyes closed.

Okay, the man said. We'll go to the aquarium first, Ms. Thompson. But then you'll be coming to the station, and after that, we may need to do a home inspection. We'll be calling in family services, and having a doctor examine your daughter. No conversation is finished until we say it's finished.

Grow some decency, my mother said. Try to be a human.

You're not allowed to insult us, the policewoman said.

I can do whatever I want. I'm the mother of a twelve-year-old girl. Even the governor is a pedophile if I say he is. And what about you? Do you like little girls?

Okay, that's enough, the policeman said. It's going to be a long day for you. But we need to go to the aquarium now. It's already after three. You'll follow us and pull over when we do, a few blocks from the aquarium. Then Caitlin will walk ahead alone, the way she usually does, and we'll be watching.

What happens if he does something before you arrive?

We already have plainclothes officers inside. Your daughter will be safe.

We drove then down East Yesler Way toward Puget Sound, dark water low beneath the city. My mother was talking fast, worried. You can't ever say I slapped you. They'll take you away from me. They'll take you away, Caitlin. I'm so sorry. I never should have slapped you, and I never will again. I promise. But you can't say anything to them. Do you understand?

I won't say anything, I said. I was starting to cry again at the thought of losing my mother.

I'm scared of them, Caitlin. They can do anything. It doesn't have to make any sense. You can't tell them anything about me. But this old man, you have to tell them everything about him. He wants to take you away too.

Our old car charging ahead like some bull, my mother rough on the accelerator and brake, panicking, the patrol car in front. The sky white and without drizzle at the moment but the streets wet. I felt like everything was ending, all put under pressure, collapsing. The sky itself would fall in, and the streets fold and submerge and the water rush in, the weight of the entire Pacific.

The most terrible betrayal. We pulled to the curb and I was standing on the sidewalk, surrounded by shallow puddles, dark mirrors, all the land pocked with holes. I could hardly walk.

Just say hello to him the way you normally would, the policeman said. Gun and baton, silver in his belt and badge, liquid that he somehow wore.

I had no choice. All set in motion. All of childhood like that. So I walked my usual route on a day unlike any other, and I could no longer gauge distance. My feet slapping down too hard or not reaching far enough. And my friend waiting, thinking he was meeting my mother today.

I wanted to flatten, my body become a gray porous crust like the pavement, my arms fins of gravel, eyes disguised as puddles. The police would walk over my body and not know. They would search and never find me. At night, I might shift along the street, feeding on whatever gathered in gutters, and I would soften in the sun, shift my coloring to a lighter gray, then darken again in rain.

But instead I was uncamouflaged, exposed for all to see, held upright, walking on legs that seemed impossible, scissoring along the sidewalk in a side-to-side wobble pinned by gravity. The aquarium now in view.

I looked behind, and the police were there half a block back, and my mother.

My heart a low thudding, heavy and far away, dread. I should have screamed a warning and run away, but I kept walking, and then I was opening the door.

The lobby, only a few people, and I wondered which ones were the police. I hesitated, thought if I just stayed here and never went into the corridors, they'd never find him. But I walked into the warm darkness, all the worlds lit on either side, and I found him at a tank with sea anemones and clownfish.

So soft, he said. Imagine living like that.

The yellow clownfish with a single white stripe along their backs. Fish that always belonged.

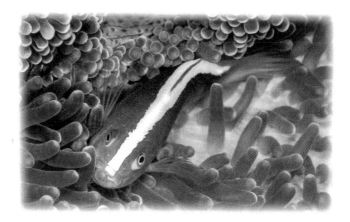

Anemones are jellyfish that never swim free, I said.

Wow, the old man said. What else?

If you touch them, it's like hundreds of little harpoons exploding, each one poisonous. That's what makes them feel sticky. But the clownfish aren't hurt.

The old man put his arm around me. Caitlin, today I have a wonderful surprise for you.

I could smell aftershave. He was wearing a new jacket

and shirt, his hair cut and combed neatly. He was smiling, nervous, his eyes twitching.

Sir, a man said from behind us. Step away from the girl. Seattle police.

What? The old man didn't understand. Three men now, plainclothes officers.

I'm sorry, I tried to say, but I couldn't speak. I couldn't breathe.

What is this?

Please step over here, sir. We'd like to ask you a few questions.

The men like shadows in their dark clothing, only their faces lit by the tanks. They were taking him away from me, but I followed. I grabbed on to his arm. Please, I said.

Who are you? the old man demanded of the men. He sounded frightened.

Seattle police.

One of the officers took my arm and pulled me away.

You've misunderstood, the old man said. No. This isn't right. You've misunderstood.

Caitlin! my mother said, loud over everything else, and she was running toward me.

Sheri! the old man said. Tell them who I am.

My mother stopped as if she had hit a wall. No, she said. She put her hands up to her face, as if she were praying, and then she fell down to her knees. No, she said. You can't do this to me.

The police were still pulling the old man away.

Sheri! he yelled. You have to tell them now. They think I'm some pervert.

He's her grandfather, my mother said. He's my father.

The police let go of him then. Caitlin, he said.

No, my mother said. You stay away from her.

My grandfather froze, as if my mother could command all.

I still want to press charges, my mother said. He wanted to take her away to Mexico. Isn't that child abduction? Or can we keep him away, maybe a restraining order?

My mother was still on her knees. The uniformed officers beside her now.

The policeman was slow in his response, his mouth open as he considered. Okay, he said. We can interview your father now. Then we'll go from there.

Sheri, the old man said. Please. He walked toward her but the police grabbed him again. Sheri. He stopped struggling, went slack, had his head down. I'm sorry. I'm sorry for everything. But don't do this now.

Like eggs in tight clusters, the most dense of the anemones. A velvet-green moon at the end of each stalk, swaying in current. Lit from within, impossible to locate. There and not there. Some buoyant sense within me, being part of a family now, belonging. The police had separated us, and the policewoman I hated was questioning me again, but I only watched the anemones and thought of all the times we would have together at every birthday, every Sunday, every day after school at the aquarium. My own grandfather. The most wondrous gift of my life.

You will tell me, the woman said.

Body of an anemone only some white constellation in the background, hidden and appearing and hidden again. I couldn't say what jellyfish or anemones were made of.

When were you going to Mexico? What was the plan?

My grandfather in some other corridor, out of sight, my mother removed also. My mother become strange, something I couldn't understand.

Mexico, Caitlin. Focus. Look at me.

But the woman didn't dare touch me. I watched the clownfish slide among the moons, all leaning in, and I knew to say nothing. Close against the glass, my own shadow face, one world hidden within another. And what would I call my grandfather? Grandpa? Or use his name, and what was his name, and where had he been all these years?

Like clusters of planets, lit by softer suns. Planets huddling together, without orbits, swaying together in some invisible current, no celestial wind but a force magnetic, scattering all and aligning again. Scale lost whenever I stared into a tank. Each universe opening.

Caitlin, did he try to kiss you?

I put my lips against the glass and kissed, held in place. My lips the base of an anemone, the foot attaching to rock. My head swaying slowly with those strange arms, my hair come alive, clownfish sliding in and tickling my scalp.

Caitlin! the policewoman said. She snapped her fingers close to my face, but all sound was deadened, submerged. Would he live with us? Would we go somewhere to live with him?

Did he make you touch him? Did he open his pants?

I closed my eyes for a while and just clung to the glass with my lips and hands. I thought of the handfish and their red painted lips, guarding their golden eggs. A garden of purple seagrass, my own small cave in the rock.

The glass was warm. A faint vibration, a humming, and this policewoman lost, floating away.

My mother arrived finally, her hand on my back. I let go of the glass and collapsed into her.

I'm sorry, Caitlin, she said.

I looked for my grandfather as we entered the lobby. Where is he? I asked.

Shh, she said.

I collapsed down to the floor. No, I said. I'm not leaving without him.

Caitlin!

Are you going to hit me?

Evelyn was not far away, near the doors. The police, also. My voice not loud, but perhaps loud enough. My mother knelt close and whispered. Caitlin, we have to be careful. I'll never hit you again, okay? But we have to be careful. And you don't know about your grandfather. You don't know what he did to me and my mother.

I'm not leaving without him.

You're never going to see him again, Caitlin. I'm sorry.

I hate you.

My mother broke then. It was very strange, something I'd never seen before. She broke completely, curling onto the carpet beside me, her arms around me, sobbing. Her entire body convulsing. The police came near, tried to speak with her, but she didn't stop, and she wouldn't let go of me. I was drowning in her, my arm trapped against her face and slick with tears. Her breath shaking, as if she were being crushed. All sound pinched and frightened.

Ms. Thompson. It was the uniformed cop. He kept trying to talk with her.

I was being pulled back into her, convulsions of a reverse birth, her mouth strained open. I was scared of her. The desperate way she clung, her shaking.

Ms. Thompson, we have to talk with you. You have to calm down. We can't hold your father. There's no evidence he had any plan to take your daughter to Mexico. It was only one comment about manta rays, about a nice place to go someday. He says he was thinking of you. A family vacation. The three of you, and he would pay. He said he asked to meet you today, that you've been estranged for many years. This is not police business. This is something you have to work out in your family. He also says he touched your daughter's chest only once, because she was panicking and he was worried, and this matches the description your daughter gave.

My mother shaking her head, rubbing in hard against me. No words but only these terrible sobs that came fast and hard, almost like hiccups.

We aren't going to hold him. Can you hear me? I'm not going to bother you anymore today. You've wasted enough of our time. Don't drive your car until you can pull it together, okay?

My mother kept crying, until long after they left. It was just the two of us on that carpet in the middle of the lobby.

The people at the aquarium too afraid to come closer, my grandfather nowhere, though I kept looking for him. The most terrifying time of my life, seeing my mother broken like that, and we needed him then.

I didn't sleep that night. Lost in darkness, aircraft over-head above the surface. Sound of them like missiles coming closer. Faint liquid light on the ceiling, underside of waves. An ocean empty, cold and without texture, unable even to mute sound. All smaller lights gone, bioluminescence a memory only, no constellations.

My grandfather. We weren't alone. What if there were other family out there too? My father, an aunt or an uncle, cousins, all hidden away by my mother, kept from me. She was still sobbing. I listened all night, and her grief came in tides. I'd think she had fallen away into sleep and then she'd begin again. She said things, small cries in anger and pain, but I never understood. I was too young for any of it. What I remember most is the fear. Everything too much. My blanket a thin covering, no protection at all.

Slow morning, gray and watery light, sound of rain. We rose only to use the bathroom, and she called in sick to work. Otherwise we remained in our separate beds. No school. No Shalini. No aquarium. My stomach growling and knees sore from shifting onto my side. I somehow finally fell asleep and woke late in the afternoon.

Mom? I called out. I had this panic that she was gone.

But she came in and lay down next to me, facing each other like sea horses. Her eyes red and cheeks and lips puffy, hair tangled.

I love you, sweet pea, she said.

I know.

And we're going to be okay.

Do I call him Grandpa?

We don't call him anything, sweet pea. He left long ago, so he doesn't get to come back.

I was too tired to fight my mother. She had an arm over me, and I just watched her eyes and mouth.

You know I don't talk about the past, my mother said. But I'm going to tell you. You need to know. My mother was dying. His wife. And he left. Just disappeared and we never heard from him. He ran away. This was when I was just starting high school, only a couple years older than you. I took care of my mother, so I didn't finish school. I had to drop out. I never went to college, never got to have my life. He took that away. And now I have the worst jobs a person can have, with no money and no future. We'll be okay, and you don't need to worry, but I won't be able to become anything. Do you understand?

I nodded.

You don't really understand, she said. You have to be older. But you can study fish. That can be your life, your job. If you do all your homework, you can be a scientist or anything else. You can decide.

Grandpa said I could be an ichthyologist.

My mother squeezed my arm then, too hard, and shook it.

You're hurting me, I said.

He doesn't get to do this. He doesn't get to see you or tell you anything.

Stop it! You're hurting me.

My mother let go. She got up fast from the bed and walked out, slapping the wall hard with her open hand then disappearing.

I had never seen this violent side of my mother before. It was terrifying, as if someone else had been living inside her all along, some darker self. I didn't feel safe.

She fixed lunch by destroying things. Slamming the pan onto the stovetop. Chopping vegetables with what sounded like an axe, attacking the wooden cutting board. I didn't dare go out and look. I stayed in my bed and flinched when she banged pots and pans.

The worst part of childhood is not knowing that bad things pass, that time passes. A terrible moment in childhood hovers with a kind of eternity, unbearable. My mother's anger extending infinitely, a rage we'd never escape. She had always been my safety, the two of us piled together on the bed whenever we arrived home, rolling over to crush me but only in play, the same as two clown loaches stacked on top of each other, looking out from their cave. To have this place become unsafe left nowhere else.

I always fix the lunch or dinner or whatever it is, my mother yelled out. Since I was fourteen. Fourteen years old. That's when I became responsible for everything. Cooking, cleaning, shopping, nursing, trying to make enough money. A shack by the road. That's what he left us in. No car. No health insurance. No job. No money. The hospital would take her when she was bad enough but not all the other times. All the other times were my special treat, my little fuck you from the world, drowning in blood and shit and piss and vomit. And then he shows up to be grandpapa. How cute.

I couldn't touch this other time, couldn't reach back to make my grandmother real. No more than a story. My mother's anger had no source I could believe.

Why don't we just start with the day he left? my mother yelled. We'll count from there, all the days he was gone, and then you can see him after that. You'll be about thirty, and you can go get an ice cream cone together. Or maybe he'll be dead, hopefully, and you can visit his grave. I'll let you know where it is, and I'll be taking a shit on it every night.

I folded my pillow over my ears, pressing in.

There's probably another family. Half brothers and half sisters of mine, right here in Seattle, or in Mexico, or on the moon. We can make enchiladas out of moon cheese. What the hell is he thinking? That we'll all go on a picnic?

I hid as long as I could, but finally she called me out for

lunch or dinner or whatever it was. Sitting at the table but staring up at the ceiling, her arms folded.

My mother looked old. Dark moons under her eyes, hair wild, dirty creases in her skin. Mouth hung downward.

Our food was a kind of omelet with things chopped up in it. Zucchini, celery, apple, lunchmeat. It wasn't normal food.

Eat, she said. A family meal.

I could see eggshells, shards of white.

Want some ketchup? she asked in a bright voice.

I nodded.

She went to the fridge and brought back the squeeze bottle. She held it out with one arm about three feet over my omelet and squeezed. Most of it landed on my plate, some on the table.

Oops, she said. Maybe Grandpa will clean that up for us. We can always count on good old Grandpa.

I was trying not to cry.

Oh, is little Boopsie upset? My mother put her face in close to mine. Welcome to my life. You have nothing to cry about. Let me tell you a little story. Your mother is the star.

My mother grabbed both my arms, hard, her smile savage, looking like another person, some stranger I'd never met.

Your mother is older, probably sixteen now, and her mother is close to the end of this long dying that goes on forever. This is the story of the blood egg.

I don't want to hear.

But you're going to hear.

You're hurting me.

That's right. So you'll pay some attention. So your mother has just washed her mother, given her a nice bath, all clean and good and there's even a smile from her mother. It's late at night, but finally all is good, and your mother can rest. She's so tired. She's not going to school anymore, but just taking care of her mother is exhausting like you wouldn't believe. So she lays her in bed, with clean sheets, which is rare. It's a special moment. And that's when the blood egg happens. It's just there suddenly, between her mother's legs, on the white sheet, dark red and thick, almost black, and soaking so quickly into the white sheet and the mattress, this lighter red spreading. And your mother doesn't know where the egg has come from or if it has to be put back. It's just too confusing. It can't be real, and yet there it is.

Please stop, I said, but she wouldn't let me go.

So your mother scoops up the blood egg in her hands, so it won't keep soaking into the bed. She's afraid the entire bed will be taken over, all turned to blood. She can see that. In her life, that kind of thing is possible. The entire house could be swallowed. There are no limits. And her mother is lying there peacefully. She doesn't even know the blood egg has happened. And how can that be? How can that come from her and she not know?

My mother looked away from me, her face softening, remembering. Her grip on my arms not so hard.

It was so large, it filled both my hands, and so thick it could have been a heart, and I just didn't know what to do with it. I didn't want it to be there, but it kept being there, and finally I walked outside and laid it carefully on the dirt under a small tree. I still don't know what it was. But this is when we needed my father. Can you understand? I needed to have another parent, an adult, but there was no one. He left.

I lay awake that night thinking of my mother, this other life, a shadow of my own. Terrible weight of a debt unpayable. What do we owe for what has come before us, the previous generations? I had no words for this at twelve, only the weight. And I think of it still. That sense of my own life held in arrest until my mother and her mother can be compensated. I don't know if it's just, only that it is.

The problem is that we can never enter this shadow world in order to make payment. We can't get there or even believe it. My grandmother lying in her bed dying. And what of her life before her dying? Who was she then? I'd have to know that time, too, in order to know what has to be restored.

I lay awake and tried to see her, but I could see only my mother's face. I couldn't make my grandmother anything except the same. And so my own mother seemed already to have died and been there as nurse at her own dying and now lived again. And was I any different or only this same woman's future?

The dead reaching for us, needing us, but this isn't true. There's only us reaching for them, trying to find ourselves.

In the morning, we rose in darkness, my mother looking destroyed. She poured cereal and some went on the counter and she seemed not to notice. We ate at the table with only the small light from over the sink. Darkness and shadow, teeth chewing and nothing else moving, the way I imagined all the tanks after the aquarium closed. I'd seen the light go out in one of the small tanks for freshwater fish, the green plants gone black and the fish the same, water clear as air unseen and only a brief moment of reflection, scales caught in light, then turned and vanished again. A world erased.

We drove toward the great lights, pulled north, all shapes lit only along their edges, outlined in silver, railcars and overhead wires and bridges not yet fully made. Returning to a normal day but with no sense anymore of what that was. Would I see the old man at the aquarium after school?

We slid up to Gatzert, the curb empty, no one else in sight, no movement. I'll pick you up right here, my mother said. I don't know what time. Maybe five, maybe later. I have to make up for yesterday.

I want to go to the aquarium.

No. You'll meet me right here.

She was gone then, and I was left alone under a sky still black and without stars. The air cold and wet even without rain. I wondered if I could walk to the aquarium after school, see my grandfather, and get back in time for my mother not to know.

I knocked on the glass doors, and the janitor let me in. An old man who didn't speak English. A kind of ghost. Blue coveralls and a face hidden away. After opening the door, he walked somehow without sound down a hallway and disappeared into a room. What was his life? Awake all night alone in these hallways, sleeping during the day. What was left? Sometimes adult life seemed unbearably sad. My mother's work that meant nothing and would lead nowhere and took most her time, my grandfather on his own pulled away by police, my grandmother dying. I wanted all of the sadness to stop and everyone to just come together.

I sat on my bench and waited, tried to look at my homework but was so exhausted I lay down and fell asleep. Heaviest of sleeps, but I woke to the bell that signaled ten minutes until class. Shalini not here yet. Drool on my backpack. Kids everywhere, shouting and laughing that somehow hadn't pulled me awake earlier. I sleepwalked to the bathroom to pee and then was back in the hallway and finally she arrived, smiling and throwing her arms around me, most delicious of feelings, smell of her and heat of her and softness and this thumping in my chest and I could have remained like that for hours but a teacher pushed us along toward our room and we had to sit apart.

Mr. Gustafson was calling us people. Listen, people, we're in the second week of December. We have only the rest of this week, which is passing fast, and a couple days next week and that's it. Everything has to be finished. Do you understand? We're not going to have time for math or English or anything else, unfortunately, so you can leave your books at home. Now let's get to work.

Lakshmi Rudolph still needed legs, but we were working on her belly. Long strips curving, and we stood over her with our foreheads pressed together, arms reaching below. Shalini's hands over mine, our fingers slick with paste and sliding. I closed my eyes and just kept running my hands along the curves. Sound of her breathing.

What the hell is this? Mr. Gustafson asked. I can't even say what that looks like.

So don't look, Shalini said.

We're going to have a talk with your parents, Shalini. You're developing an attitude problem.

I'm sorry I'm not excited enough about Christmas. I'm sure my parents will want to remedy that.

Jesus Christ. You're only eleven or twelve.

Twelve.

I shouldn't have to be dealing with this shit yet. You're going to be a nightmare in junior high.

I'd rather do math than make a paper-mache reindeer. That's a bad attitude. You're right.

Fine. Do your own Jello pool thing and ignore the rest of the world.

Thank you, Baba Gustafson. Shalini bowed to him and smiled as he left. In India, my teachers were tougher.

America is too easy.

I have a grandfather.

What?

The old man at the aquarium is my grandfather.

No.

Yes.

Shalini gave me a hug, both of us pressed in close to Lakshmi Rudolph, getting paste on our shirts. You have a family now, she said.

At snack break, we went out behind the baseball backstop and lay down in the gravel. I was on my back, Shalini on top of me. Her tongue fluttering around mine, the sky white above her, as if she were some giant descended to pin me down to the earth. Pulse of her, and our breath ragged. Her lips so soft.

I could not pull her close enough, and the break was so short, instantly over. We had to run to class.

The sleigh had grown, puffy and misshapen, a children's playhouse on skids. Near it, an enormous dreidel with a point made from wire hangers. It would never spin. Along the back wall, the long skin of a dragon and its spiky head with a large red tongue. Most of its brown canvas still showing, all needing to be painted. Two other reindeer, with wire horns and knobby legs, two elves with green slippers, and a Santa. Our Rudolph was the only piece of Diwali. No elephants, no goddesses with many arms. Hundreds of Hindu gods, all represented by Rudolph.

This is ridiculous, I said.

Come here, Shalini said. She pulled me behind Rudolph and kissed me. We were in the back of the room, and if we crouched down and hid behind his belly, no one could see us. Mr. Gustafson was looking at his book of classic cars, which was what he did when he felt overwhelmed.

Shalini held my head in both hands and pulled me in closer and closer, but I was afraid, so I backed away and stood up.

You don't have to worry, she said. Everyone is in a panic. Look at them.

It was true. The room was total chaos, so loud I could hardly hear her.

Shalini scrunched her nose and snorted, and she raised her eyebrows, eyes wide.

I laughed. Mr. Gustafson's eyebrows were always raised as he looked down at his book, the classic cars continually amazing, and his nose did seem almost to quiver, snuffling for something tasty.

After school, I was running. I'd thrown my backpack behind some bushes. Enormous white-gray sky, heavy, the air like milk. Fear of being caught by my mother. The land jagged as I ran, all shaken on impact, skyscrapers tilted and tossed.

Cars passing beside me, drifting away, this street unbearably long, endless apartments and houses and businesses. A city holds all that we want and a million times what we don't want.

You have to be there, I thought. Please be there.

I burst through the front doors out of breath, sweaty, and

had to throw off my coat. The aquarium staff not saying hello, only watching. After our scene, they didn't want to come anywhere near me.

I used the drinking fountain and waited for my breath and heart to calm. I was looking down the dark hallway but didn't see him.

I dragged my jacket and walked slowly down the corridor. I was early, so it was possible he hadn't yet arrived, or he could have been looking at the fish. At the first fork, I didn't know which way to go, but I decided against the larger, brighter displays and sea mammals. I decided to go toward the darker hallways, the nocturnal fish and deep-sea dwellers, and I found him here. Dark tank of black sand and dirt, no rock, nowhere to hide. My grandfather leaned in close to the glass, peering at the ocellated waspfish, one of my favorites. It looked like a moth, pale yellow-green wings and a head that could have been covered in white fuzz. Thin white feelers like insect legs. And then the body of a fish, as if the two had been grafted together, some transformation in darkness unexplained, two worlds that should never have touched.

So beautiful, I said.

Caitlin, he said, and he rushed to hug me, pulled me in close against him. Rough sound of his breath and beating of his heart. Dry skin of his hand cradling my head. I wrapped my arms around him. Grandpa, I said.

Odd ridges and folds of him beneath his shirt, smell of laundry and deodorant and someone old. He was the same as home, as belonging.

I love you, Caitlin.

I love you too, Grandpa.

We just held each other for the longest time. I closed my eyes. Swaying a bit, as if we were in a warm current, our own lagoon somewhere in the Marshall Islands or Indonesian archipelago.

I'm so sorry, Caitlin. That was an awful thing on Monday. You shouldn't have had to see that. But things will get better now. It may take a long time for your mother to forgive me, but things will get better.

I held him as tightly as I could.

It was such a shock to see your mother up close. She looks the same, just older.

She won't let me see you.

The old man took a big breath and sighed. He let go of me and straightened back up and looked at the waspfish. I don't blame her, he said. My baby, and I left her. And left her mother. If I could go back, I would.

I didn't know what to say. It was hard not to think of him as the old man, and he was suddenly far away. I watched the waspfish cruising just over the bottom in dim light, white feelers exploring, searching for food, for anything buried.

It was just unbearable, he said. Something in me couldn't stay. I couldn't watch my wife dissolve into nothing. The terrible part was the helplessness. I couldn't do anything to make her well.

I didn't want to listen. It was too much, hearing my mother and then my grandfather. I only looked at the waspfish. Folding those pale green wings, then opening them again at any threat, any sense of someone watching behind the glass or a larger shape coming from above. That black sand and dirt should have been the continental shelf, extending out hundreds of miles from New York, and this fish cruising right to the edge, to the drop-off.

Did you know waspfish bury themselves in sand during the day, with only their eyeballs poking out? he asked me. He always knew when I was panicking. He always knew how to calm me.

Yeah, I said. But they're never in less than fifty feet of water, and usually deeper, so it's not much light. I don't really see the difference.

Good point. I guess you learn a certain range in your life. What looks like no change at all to us is day and night for him. And the cold. It's always cold where he is, but he might feel a change as something enormous.

Like us now.

That's right, like us now. You're smart, Caitlin.

He put his arm around me and I leaned into him.

My life has had a narrow range for too long, he said.

The waspfish made a quick dash and then turned and opened her wings. I kept expecting her to flutter and break free of that fish half and rise through water become air.

Do you know how deep this tank is? I asked.

No.

It's forty feet deep.

No.

It stacks up way above us to provide pressure for the fish. If she turns into a moth, she has to swim up forty feet before she's free.

I love that. I can see her become a moth and rise up toward the light. And you're right, it's not a he.

The tank wasn't really forty feet high, but I liked to think it was, and I was happy he believed me. I imagined the back rooms like Willy Wonka's chocolate factory, a bright land of colorful pipes and bubbles and pumps. I knew it wasn't like that, of course, but I wanted it to be.

We drifted on to a tank that was a bubble, dark and under pressure, with king crabs. My grandfather's arm around my shoulders. Smooth stones, almost black, and this red spiky armor, white underneath.

It looks like someone put it together piece by piece, I said. You can see all the joints.

It seems impossible it could grow, my grandfather said. To begin small with all those same plates, and all the plates grew and still fit.

One of the crabs was reaching high on the glass toward us, legs three feet long outstretched. Underside of its body like fingers interlocked, which looked as if they might open and some other creature emerge.

I can see myself in the fish, my grandfather said, but not in the crabs.

Me either. Those tiny eyes on stalks have nothing behind them. And that mouth. You can't call that a mouth. It's just more legs.

He laughed. I feel so lucky to be with you, Caitlin. I wish this aquarium could go on and on for miles, with every fish and crab and other strange thing in the sea.

He pulled me even closer against him, and I was so happy I couldn't speak. The king crab would never know this feeling.

You're right that it's the mouth, he said. If it had lips, we'd feel closer to it. All we need are eyes and lips, apparently, and we think we can say hello. I don't think I realized that before, how much we need the world to look like us.

My grandfather drove me back to school in a very old Mercedes. Everything polished, as if new, as if we were going back in time.

I like your car, I said. My mother drives a Thunderbird.

He smiled. I know. I had to find the two of you, so I've seen where you live, and Sheri's car, and where she works. Please don't tell her that. She'll be angry. But I wanted to find you.

Okay, I said, but I didn't know what to think of that. How long had he been watching us?

I'm a mechanic, he said. Or was. I'm retired now. But I worked on diesel engines all my life. This is a diesel. Can you hear the difference in sound?

I listened, but I couldn't really tell. Maybe, I said.

Well listen to the Thunderbird again. It'll sound smoother, like all one sound when your mother accelerates. The diesel is like hearing pins, and if there's a turbo, you hear that over the top after the acceleration, as it winds down. Almost like an airplane. This one isn't a turbo.

He accelerated then and I listened. It did sound like pins. It sounds like it could break, I said.

Ah, it lasts much longer. I can go a million miles on this engine, and I can also run it for a week, if I want, without turning it off. Day and night. No gas engine can do that.

Wow.

Engines have lives, like people. If something happens, some sign of that remains, always. There's history in an engine. I'll be with this engine until the end.

What do you mean, the end?

Sorry, Caitlin. I meant my end, but it's not coming soon, I promise. There's nothing to worry about. I'll be here for you.

I felt like crying suddenly, but I just stared out my side window and held it back, and soon enough we were at Gatzert.

I'm sorry, Caitlin. I didn't mean to upset you. He took off his seat belt and leaned across the bench seat to hug me. I clung to his arm, which was thick and strong, I noticed now, from his work. And thank you for coming to see me. I'll be there every day, and we'll figure out something with your mother. She just needs time.

I found my backpack in the bushes and sat on a metal bench by the front doors. Sunset, maybe, the light still from nowhere but less of it now. I was bundled up, but it was cold, so I went inside and waited there. Eternal light in long tubes. I don't think they ever turned off. Just flicked on once until they died and were replaced. So maybe not eternal.

It was fully dark when my mother arrived. And she was tired. How are you, sweet pea? she murmured.

Okay, I said. How was work?

Oh, just more of the same. I could miss every day of work, never go back, and it would all still be the same there. I don't have any effect. Just doing time.

It was rare my mother was like this. Only when she was really tired.

Steve is coming over, fixing dinner right now. I hope that's okay.

Yeah, I said. I like Steve.

Yeah. He's a good guy.

We drove the rest the way in silence, and I realized I was hiding now, without meaning to. Only a few days earlier, I could have talked with her about anything, but now everything important had to be kept secret. I couldn't tell her I'd seen my grandfather, couldn't talk about his life or ask questions, couldn't share what we'd seen or said at the aquarium. And I couldn't talk about kissing Shalini, about my entire life changing in every way. And this had all happened in four days.

I listened every time my mother accelerated, the smooth blow of it, different from the diesel, but I couldn't say anything. Slow swing of the shocks as we floated on.

I could smell oil frying when we opened the door. Buongiorno, Steve called. He was wearing a white chef's hat and a red-checkered apron, grinning at us.

Holy moly, my mother said.

Benvenuti, he said. Welcome to Italia and eggplant parmigiana, for the little vegetarian.

My mother laughed and squeezed up against him for a kiss. She stole his hat and wore it herself.

Are you even Italian? I asked.

No, he said with an Italian accent. But in Italy, they know good food. He had his thumb and two fingers pressed together, swinging his hand in the air.

What are you? I asked. Where do you come from?

Origins, Steve said. They don't explain us, you know. They never do. Each of us is our own piece of work. I come from Nintendo. That was one of my parents, my mother. I suckled at the controller. And AC/DC, a late but good set of fathers, Back in Black and shaking me all night long, a good precursor to Nirvana.

But where do you come from?

You're a tough nut. The old country, you want, Steve said in an Italian accent again. Well, it's Albania, right across the water from Italy, but I was never there. I've heard about beautiful mountains on the coast, olive orchards to make your heart ache, calls to prayer in the minarets, the best food this world has ever tasted, but I've tasted it only a bit from my grandparents. My parents served Oscar Mayer. So there you go. We don't come from anywhere.

I didn't know any of that, my mother said. She punched Steve in the shoulder. You don't tell me anything, and then you tell my daughter?

She's tough, your daughter. I'm afraid of her.

My mother laughed. That's true. She is tough. I'm scared of her too.

Steve was turning the slices of eggplant, breaded and browned and crackling in the oil. He had a pot of water boiling for the pasta, and a big bowl of tomato sauce. I was so happy I felt like I would pop.

Where is Albania exactly? my mother asked.

Ah, poor Albania. No one knows where it is.

Sorry.

You know how Italy is a boot?

Yeah.

Albania could get kicked by the heel of that boot. There's a bit of Greece there, too, the Ionian Islands. I want to go someday. We come from a village near the Roman ruins of Butrint, which are supposed to be really amazing. Huge stone walls and an ancient theater and the largest, best mosaic in the world, a large circular floor all done in small colored tiles, with pillars all around.

It sounds beautiful.

Yeah, I have to admit, I do sometimes wish I had grown up there.

Why? I asked.

Steve was pulling all the eggplant from the pan now and putting it in a large casserole dish with tomato sauce. History, he said. To stand in a place and know that this is where you come from for a dozen generations, or maybe a hundred generations, or maybe more. To know there was a great city two thousand years ago in this place, and that your ancestors helped build it and lived there and worked there. When you walk down a small road, all the others who are walking there with you from before.

Steve put a final layer of sauce over the top and then picked up a hunk of hard parmesan and a grater. My mother hugged him from behind. I better enjoy you now, she said. Sounds like someone is leaving for Albania.

Sadly that never happens. We never go back.

You should, I said. At least to visit. You have to.

Steve laughed. Okay, then. Commanded. Now it will happen.

He grated the cheese over the top and then put the casserole dish in the oven. Twenty minutes, he said.

Why don't you go lie down, my mother said to me. You look tired.

So I went to my room to leave them alone. I lay on my bed with the lights out and looked for shapes on the ceiling. Curtain light, bent into waves by the folds. Passing cars like shortened days, rising and falling. I was exhausted and overwhelmed and had no thoughts.

I woke disoriented. Hungry. I struggled to rise and cross the floor and found them at the table, the dinner dishes stacked on the counter. You didn't wake me, I said.

No, sweet pea, you looked so tired.

But I missed dinner.

It's still here, Steve said. I'll serve you right up. He put his hat back on, stood and waved me over to a seat, said, Bella, prego, and served me a plate of eggplant parmesan on pasta, with a bit of salad on the side. Buon appetito, he said.

I felt half asleep still, groggy and lost. I took a bite with my fork and it was only warm, not hot, but it was good. I have a grandfather, I said.

What's that? Steve asked.

Stop, Caitlin, my mother said.

She said she has a grandfather?

Yes, my mother said. My father decided to reappear after nineteen years to play grandpa.

Wow.

I met him at the aquarium.

You didn't meet him. He tracked us down. He's old and lonely now, probably dying and needs a nurse, and since I have such great practice at being a nurse, why not me? Or he feels like a miserable fuck for what he's done and now he wants to be forgiven.

Nineteen years, Steve said. That's a long time.

Since Caitlin wants to bring you into this, you might as well know he left me to take care of my dying mother. Left us alone with nothing. When I was fourteen.

I couldn't eat the eggplant. I was just staring down, pulling it apart with my fork. The dark ribbon around each piece hidden under bread crumbs, soft yellow meat with darker swirls, camouflage, swimming in a thick red sea. Lying flat on the bottom, hidden away.

Why did you want me to know? Steve asked quietly.

So you can help, I said.

Oh, this is beautiful. My mother threw her arms in the air. Thank you both. This is great. Because I've been such a bad person, and my father is such an angel.

No, Steve said. No. I wasn't trying to say anything.

Well Caitlin is. Caitlin told me she hates me. I want Grandpa.

My mother said it in a whining, baby voice, making fun of me. Then she reached over and knocked on my forehead. Knock, knock, she said. You don't have a fucking grandpa.

Sheri, Steve said.

Get out. Get the fuck out.

Steve looked down, slumped, and we all just waited, silent. I could hear our clock and my mother's breathing. I could feel my forehead where her knuckles had been.

Then Steve rose and grabbed his jacket and walked out. No good-bye, and he didn't even turn around to look at us.

My mother pounded the table with her fist, my plate jumping. Is this what you want? she asked, her mouth all twisted up. To take everything away from me? You want me to just work and that's it? No life?

No.

Well then. Wake the fuck up. You get me or him. Not both.

I burrowed under my blankets and curled into a ball, like a lungfish waiting for rain. Hibernation, but called estivation, since it's for the hot summer instead of cold winter. When everything is unbearable and exposure too much, the air too hot to breathe. My mother the best person in this world, the most generous, the strongest, but this was her dry season, when she was more like a storm than a person, wind-blown dust, accelerating from somewhere sourceless and vast, and I knew to hide.

Lungfish can slow to one-sixtieth their normal metabolic rate, but this slows time, also. One night becomes sixty nights. This is the price for hiding. Just hold your breath for one minute and find out what a minute becomes.

In the morning, I tried to remain invisible. I looked down at my cereal and never looked up. My chewing took forever. We ate again with only the small light from over the sink, which made night shadows of everything, large and distorted.

He has nothing to lose, my mother said. This whole game costs him nothing. I pay, but he doesn't pay. Same as it's always been.

I knew not to say anything. Anything I said would be an attack. I looked up only in quick glances, my mother's face in shadow, hidden, the light behind her.

And what you don't know is that things can be lost quickly. I can lose Steve, and it only takes a few nights like last night. Only a few, and it won't matter everything we did together before. All of that can be erased. All you have to do is hold out a little longer and you'll take him away from me. Do you want that? No more Steve?

I'm not trying to do anything.

You can cut that crap, too. You know what you're doing. You haven't listened to anything I've said about the past. You don't care what he did to me. And don't start crying. I'm sick of that whole self-pity thing. Your life is easy. We have to go now anyway or we'll be late. And do you know why we have to go so early?

I wasn't looking at her. I looked at my bowl of cereal and tried not to hear.

We're going because your mother gets to be a slave all

her life, so that the little princess can have a better life. This is what parents do.

Parent, I said. One parent.

Oh, that's beautiful. So you really do want to fight.

I tried to do better than the lungfish. I tried to burrow down and turn to stone. No hole of dried mud to emerge from at the first rains, but my body turned to rock.

You're not going to say anything more? Just that little gem and that's it?

I thought my mother would hit me, but she didn't. She stalked away and grabbed her stuff and opened the door. We're going now.

I was tempted to stay. What would happen if I just didn't move? But I was afraid of her, so I stood up, grabbed my backpack and coat, and slid past her out the door.

Cold, snowing, cones of yellow flakes in the streetlights pressing downward and come from nowhere, only black above. I held the handrail in case of ice. I could feel the air in my nose and throat.

It's gonna be great at work, my mother said. What a pleasure to be outside in nature, with all the steel beams and slush and oil and hydraulic fluid and grime and salt sprayed everywhere, and great to know this is still the beginning, that it'll be about four more months of the same. More rain than snow, but still cold. What a great pleasure. What an honor.

My door was frozen shut, so I had to yank to break it free. My mother was scraping ice off the windshield. No one else around at this hour, the cars and apartments dark. The ground cracking beneath us. I slid in to the bench seat, my legs instantly cold through my jeans. I sat on my gloved hands and hunched over to conserve warmth. If we just sat here for a few hours and did nothing, we could die.

My mother cranked the engine, and it was slow to start. She revved it, smooth fans of power, no sound of pins. And then we drove slowly down our street onto East Marginal Way South going north, taillights of other cars ahead now and lights of the city beyond.

My favorite part, my mother said, is when I get all sweaty and then we have to wait awhile, just standing around, and the sweat freezes.

I'm sorry, I said.

Well that's a start.

But I'm not doing anything wrong.

That's maybe not as good an apology. I didn't think this was going to happen for another year, until your teens, but I guess it might as well start now. Why have another year of peace when we could fight right away?

You're the one who's making it a fight.

Yeah, my mother said. Yeah. This is the beginning. I did this to my mother, too, until she started dying. Then I wanted to cut out my nasty little tongue for everything I'd said. So what can I do to short-circuit you? Maybe tell you about your father. Would you like to hear about your father?

Yes.

I bet you would. So let's save that for a time when you're playing nice.

You've never told me anything.

That's right.

My mother flicked on the heater, the engine warm enough now, and we sat in our own small desert, blown by hot wind at our feet and in our faces while the snow fell outside. Like rain in the headlights but white and slower, suspended then caught in a rush as we collided. The lights of the city muted and blurred.

It was a long time before we reached East Yesler Way, driving up the hill into what no longer felt like a city. Gatzert waiting lit and lonely by the side of the road.

What time? I asked.

I don't know. Maybe four thirty, maybe five thirty.

She was gone then. She would be outside all day in the cold, and next winter would be the same, and the winter after that, all the years until I was her age and she would still be working, another twenty years, and another ten years after that, three more of my lifetimes, an eternity. I think that morning was the first time I understood. It was too awful to be true. My own mother trapped, a slave just as she had said.

The old janitor let me in and disappeared into his cage somewhere, and I sat under the soulless fluorescent lights and waited. This was the beginning of my mother's life, waiting and doing nothing. The cold, and we keep breathing, and that's it.

I hadn't done any homework, but I couldn't pull out the books now, and Mr. Gustafson wouldn't be checking anyway. I remembered then that he had said not to even bring the books. So I just sat and waited for an hour and a half until everyone was yelling and running and laughing and finally Shalini appeared, sleepy and soft, and she had her arms around me for about two minutes and then we had to go to class.

Mr. Gustafson had stopped trying. We wouldn't be ready for the Christmas parade—there would be unpainted parts of the dragon and sleigh, bits of wire showing in the legs and antlers of the reindeer, Lakshmi Rudolph with almost no legs at all, a formless Santa, a dreidel that would never spin—and he was tired. Every other year had probably been a failure too, and he had no plan B.

I remember being angry at Mr. Gustafson, but Shalini never was bothered. She didn't mind chaos, and she found the ridiculous funny.

Look at his tongue, she said. His tongue is out. And it was true. As he looked at his book of cars, his mouth had opened and his fat tongue was bulging out over his lower lip.

Yuck, I said.

Come over here, she said, and I knelt behind our Rudolph. I love your hair, she said. So light. It weighs nothing. She lifted my hair and kissed all along my neck and my skin tightened everywhere, goose bumps and chills. I was shivering, even though I wasn't cold. She kissed my ear and all along my jaw until she reached my lips. I wanted to breathe her in, to hold her inside, and I wanted everyone else to disappear, to just go away.

My mother won't let me see my grandpa.

Shalini kept kissing me. Don't talk, she said.

I'm worried she never will.

Shalini stopped then and opened her eyes. You saw him yesterday, didn't you? You went running off.

Yeah.

And you can see him again today?

Yeah.

Well then. Everything is okay.

But I don't want to hide and have secrets.

Caitlin, she said. Look at what we're doing now. You are going to have secrets.

I ran to my grandfather again, ran until my lungs ached in the cold and my legs felt brittle, made of glass. It was snowing still, a layer now half a foot thick and made of nothing, my feet sinking through as if the snow were only air. The city disappearing, all edges softened, the sky the same as the land. Only streetlights and windows remained, and the dark tracks cars made in the road.

I had to walk, to catch my breath. Heart pounding and skin slick with sweat under my coat. I didn't want a secret life, hidden from my mother. I couldn't imagine living that way.

There was no telling where the sun might be. The faint light an emanation that came from everywhere at once, the sea vanished, this road shortened at both ends and the sky close enough to touch. The sound of my own breath.

I ran again, but it seemed to take forever to reach the aquarium. Inside felt hot, and I stripped off my coat.

I found him at the largest tank just as a school of mackerel came at us with their mouths hung open, straining for plankton.

Look, my grandfather said. You can see right through their mouths to the water behind. Their mouths go nowhere.

I had never noticed that before. The food would never reach their stomachs. They'd be forever hungry, always eating and finding nothing. That's wrong, I said.

I don't understand it, he said. Where does it connect?

What I saw was every part of a fish wandering the oceans on its own. One of these gaping mouths straining through endless water with no body attached, a tail like a boomerang flinging itself through blue empty space, an eye floating alone. What if everything was unfinished? What if everything was made incomplete?

They're alive, my grandfather said. And they're fast swimmers, so obviously it all works out somehow, but I don't see how. And what are plankton, really? They seem made up, like fairy tale. Some huge whale skimming through nothing with an open mouth and ending up fed.

I think it's not finished, I said. I think none of it is finished.

What do you mean?

I felt overwhelmed. I don't know, I said.

I think I see what you mean, he said. We think the world is done, that this is the way it is, but it's really still making itself. In a million years, the mackerel will have some balloon opening to its stomach to match that head.

That's not what I mean, I said.

What do you mean?

That we're not put together yet. Parts are missing.

So the first version isn't done? Not that there will be other versions, but even the first one isn't yet complete?

Yeah.

Hm. I understand that. But I don't think it's true, Caitlin. I think we're okay. I think we're complete. I mean our lives are all screwed up, but I think we have everything we need.

The mackerel were far away now, at the other end of the tank, pale shadows gathering, tricks of light, no more than dust motes in air. The sea a great blindness, too thick, shapes coming into view only up close. No warning.

Cod in close now, low against the rocks and weeds, fattened and slow, yellow-brown and aimless, dull eyes.

A kind of saltwater catfish, waiting only to be eaten. The flat rounded plates of their heads, armor, thick sad lips, one white tendril for finding food in sand. Perhaps they were complete, but for what purpose?

What's that? my grandfather asked.

Cod.

Dinner. I didn't know they looked like that. They're so yellow, they make the water around them look yellow. I never would have noticed them if you hadn't been looking.

I looked up again to where the mackerel were coming around, bright silver heads gasping open, and they did make the water itself brighter, bluer, just like he said. You're right. The cod make the water look muddy and yellow.

The mackerel were so fast, kinks of light with black racing stripes, turned and gone.

Most of the fish here we don't even see, my grandfather said. Someone visits the aquarium. They look at the sharks,

see the king crab, point at the brightest colors, but most of
the fish go unnoticed, anything drab or brown, anything slow.

That's true, I said. I've never seen anyone look at the
cod for this long.

And the cod will be here forever. The mackerel look like
they're trying to escape. Like they're looking for a way out.
And they'll probably find it. But the cod don't care. They're
willing to believe this aquarium is the whole world. They're
going to have lunch or be served for lunch, and it's all the same.

I feel sorry for the cod, I said.

Me too. They just look sad. I don't think I can keep looking at them. We have to move on to something else.

I know where we can go, I said. Just upstairs. This same
tank, but the highest part, all open water. The mola mola.
Have you seen him?

I didn't know there was an upstairs.

I was so excited I felt like jumping up and down. I could
show my grandfather something new.

Let's hurry then, he said. I'm dying to see.

We walked up a narrow dark ramp with round portholes,
like a submarine. Don't look, I said. You have to close your
eyes until I say to open them.

I took my grandfather by the hand and led him up to the
small room that looked out on a deep and endless blue.
No rock formations, no seaweed, no cod or other bottom
fish, and even the mackerel and albacore and sharks made
only brief visits on their rounds. But the mola mola loved
to lie flat on the surface, open to the sky, one eye looking
upward. And then he'd submerge just below and swim all

along the edge of the tank in his unlikely, twisting way. My grandfather kept his eyes closed patiently, and I waited until the fish was right in front of us.

Open, I said.

Oh, he said. Oh my god. It's the man in the moon.

And suddenly I could see it. A crescent moon in white, and his face looking upward.

That mouth, he said. And the white eye. Not his real eye, in darkness, but that small white one just ahead forms another face. His real eye looks afraid, but with that other eye he's seeing god, looking into the heavens in rapture.

The mola mola turned and twisted away, the dark side of the moon all we could see now, dark craters and canyons fading into the deeper blue on great fins we weren't normally allowed to witness, what propels each planet and moon.

Caitlin, he said. That was nothing less than a vision. Thank you.

He pulled me close against his side, and we watched the shadow form circling, waited for its orbit to come close again.

We hurried across Alaskan Way in the snow. End of the day, diffused light, thick traffic crunching along slowly, a few tires with chains, others with studs. Endless migration. My grandfather able on his feet, maybe younger than he looked. He unlocked the passenger door for me, went around to the driver's seat. He held the key to the right and nothing happened. Glow plugs, he said. They heat the engine for twenty seconds. Then he turned the key the rest the way and the engine came to life, sounding like a tractor idling. He went out to scrape the windshield and I waited.

I wish we could stay in the aquarium, I said when he returned. He was breathing hard.

Me too.

I'd like to live there. I could have a bed in the hallway and look up at the fish before going to sleep.

I'd want to stay in that upper room with the mola mola, he said, gasping. I'd become a monk and worship with him, looking upward.

He's called the great ocean sunfish, but I like mola mola better.

Me too, my grandfather said. Mola mola sounds like the name of a god. An easy god.

We drove then, slowly up Yesler, and I didn't want to say good-bye. I wish you could come to our house, I said.

That would be wonderful. But we have to give your mother time. It was horrible that I left her, and I don't deserve to be forgiven, but I hope I will be anyway, only because I want to know you and also know her. I want to be there, part of a family. We have only this one life, so we have to hope for forgiveness.

When we arrived at Gatzert in the snow, there was a car at the curb with its lights on, my mother's car.

Oh no, I said.

It's okay. This had to happen at some point.

He parked and she stepped out in her blue coveralls, stained with oil. Another mechanic, I suddenly realized, just like him. Her head bare, hair loose and tangled.

I don't care what she says, I told my grandfather.

Caitlin, go to your mother. It's okay.

So I opened my door and stepped out with my backpack.

Get in the car, Caitlin, my mother said. She was lit up bright in the headlights and falling snow, hair wild, like some goddess of winter. And as soon as I moved, she stalked over to his car and kicked his door.

Stop, I yelled, but she kicked his door again, hard. He just sat there and watched her.

I ran around the front of his car and tried to stop her, tried to grab her arm, but she pushed me down into the road, my hands and knees wet in slush, and she kept kicking with her steel-toed boot, denting in the side of his car. Dark blue form hunched and maddened.

Stop, Mom. Please stop.

But she was beyond hearing, a thing of rage. She hopped up on his hood and jumped, the metal buckling beneath her. Enormous dents. Then she climbed onto his roof and leapt into the air with her knees high, slamming down with her boots to cave it in. A fury fallen from the sky, no less elemental than that. She was not my mother. She was something else I had never seen. The rage in her more than I ever would have imagined.

My grandfather's hands on the steering wheel still, looking at me where I crawled in the slush. He wasn't going to move. She would destroy for as long as she liked. He looked terribly sad, caves for eyes. Wearing his rain jacket and a dark blazer beneath that, and a collared shirt. Always dressed up whenever I saw him. As if he were going to church. Waiting patiently for the service to begin.

She was yelling now as she jumped and pounded. You don't get to come back, you fucker.

She jumped down to his trunk and slipped. The metal must have been icy. She fell hard onto his back windshield and slid and rolled overboard onto the pavement and slush.

Mom! I yelled.

My grandfather rolled down his window quickly. Sheri? he asked. Are you okay?

But she rose again, unhurt, one side soaked now and darker. She swung her boot high to kick in a taillight. Splintering sound of plastic and glass. Soft explosion of the bulb.

Nice of you to ask, she said. Maybe about nineteen years late. But thank you for thinking of me.

She kicked in the other taillight.

Stop! I screamed.

I hope you love this car, she said. I hope it means something to you, Daddy.

Sheri, I'm sorry.

Save it.

She walked past his open window to the front of the car and kicked at one of his headlights, but it didn't break.

Fuck, she said. Steel-toed boots. They should be enough.

She kicked again and still it didn't break.

Fuck this. She went to her open door, and I thought we were leaving, that it was over, but she popped the trunk, walked back to open it, lit up by his headlights, and pulled out the tire iron.

Please, Sheri, he said.

Good, she said. You do care.

I only watched her, same as my grandfather did. Some agreement that this was her right, or at least unstoppable. She swung the iron at his headlight and it exploded and she screamed, no words, just a primal yell, and she shattered the other headlight, also, then swung with that iron against the body of his car, going down the passenger side, and smashed the passenger window. He put up a hand to shield himself from flying glass, but otherwise he didn't move. He only waited as she caved in the next window, a great crash in that twilight and no neighbors interested, no security from the school, only the three of us left alone in the snow as she moved on to his rear window and smashed into it from both sides.

She was breathing hard, rested for a moment against his car, her arms and the tire iron on the roof.

I'm so sorry, Sheri, he said. If I could go back in time, I would. But I can help you now. I have a little bit of money, I have a house. I can be there for Caitlin and you, both of you. You can move in if you want, stop paying rent. I can watch Caitlin in the evenings so you have your freedom.

My mother stepped back and stood there with the tire iron hanging. I thought she was going to swing at him, but she smiled. That's what you think? That we'll form a happy family now? You trade the dying wife for the granddaughter and all is made well, just in time for Christmas?

She swung fast, and he lunged to his side just in time. The iron smashed the part of his window not rolled down. And you think you can use my daughter against me?

I'm sorry, he said. He was crying now, the most awful lonely sobs.

Mom, I begged.

No. You don't get to do this. She swung at his windshield, yelling with the effort, pocking holes in it, the surface jeweled in the streetlights, caving in. She yelled until the glass was destroyed and she was hitting the dashboard and steering wheel. My grandfather lying across the bench seat, invisible to me, sound only of his voice, utterly lost.

Let me tell you what's going to happen, my mother said, breathing hard. You're going to leave us alone or I will hurt you. You don't see Caitlin ever again. I will hurt you. And you live in your house with your money and you die alone. No one will be there and no one will care. You will rot in that house until the smell brings your neighbors, and then they stick you in a hole and no one is there and no one ever visits. And that's it. That's all you get.

She bashed his side mirror until it broke off and hit the pavement. Have a nice drive home.

My mother tossed her tire iron in the trunk then and slammed it shut. Caitlin, she said. Get in now.

I walked past but he didn't see me, still lying across the seat. Dash lights making an aquarium of the interior of his car, pieces of safety glass hanging in bright pebbled waves, light blue, an ocean made brittle somehow and broken, shockwave of sound or something more, sudden and devastating. And what could he do but lie on the bottom and hide?

My mother drove too quickly in the snow and slush. The temperatures low, and there could have been ice already.

It's not enough, my mother said. Even ripping off his arms would not be enough. Reaching in through his ribs to tear out his heart, that might do it. Or crushing his skull slowly in a vise so he could feel what the pressure was like. All those years, just pressure, endless pressure. You'll never know. You'll have no fucking idea, and so you'll think I'm a monster and he's a saint. But that's fine. I don't give a shit what you think. You have six more years of room and board, and then you can leave and tell me to fuck off, tell me what a crap mother I was, how you hate me and all the rest of it. I don't care.

I leaned in close to my door and looked at the houses flying by, too fast down this hill, the feel of the tires loose and sliding. Clinging to the door handle and my seat belt.

The problem is, you can't believe anything that happened before. It's just a story to you. It isn't real. You think the world began with you. But it didn't. It began with me.

My grandfather would be driving home in the snow and cold without windows. Just the cold wind, freezing, and pebbles of safety glass everywhere. Wearing his sport coat and collared shirt, this was what made it unbearably sad, I see now. An old mechanic trying to look like a gentleman. Trying to have dignity, trying to put his life in order, driving that night in the waste of a car, exposed. No headlights or taillights, and he could easily have had a collision. I was so worried I could hardly think. A dark shape drifting, waiting for impact.

If he made it home, he'd be leaving the car out to fill with snow, going inside alone. He had invited us to live with him.

You're not giving me the silent treatment, my mother said. You're going to talk with me.

She was looking over at me while she drove. On the highway now, safer than sliding down that hill.

Answer me.

Okay.

You tell me what happened. You tell me what he did when I was fourteen.

He left.

That's right. Tell me more.

He left while your mother was dying, and you had to take care of her.

That's right, but far too fast. This went on for years. Do you understand years? Every day?

It went on for years.

What was one day like? Tell me about one day.

I hated my mother then. I wanted to leave her and live with my grandfather. I wouldn't have to get up so early, I said.

What?

If we lived with him, he could take me to school later.

My mother slapped me, hit me with her open hand as I hid against the door and covered my head. You will not fucking do that to me! she yelled. Slapping at me and trying to stay in her lane, swerving.

I'd have a family! I screamed.

My mother stretched like an octopus, arms everywhere, able to slap my face and arm and leg all at the same time she held the wheel, unfurling herself in darkness, a frightening rush I couldn't escape.

We were swerving across lanes, other drivers on their horns. My face pressed against glass as I tried to get away, and we fishtailed toward the guardrail, straightened out, and slid to a stop on the shoulder.

My mother on me then as if I were prey. Grabbing my wrists and smashing me into the corner. Her leg over me, holding me down. You will tell me, she said. You will tell me what it was like. One day. I wake up in darkness, early, and what happens?

Your mother is sick.

That's right. She's been sick all night. I've been up all night. I slept an hour or two.

You have to clean up things.

That's right. What things?

Everything awful.

Yes. Everything awful. And what is my mother doing?

I don't know.

My mother shook me. Think, Caitlin. What do people do when they're dying?

I don't know.

Moaning. A lot of moaning and twisting back and forth. Screaming sometimes. Crying and self-pity. Vomiting and shitting and pissing and bleeding. Tell me what that was like.

It was too much, I said. You wanted it all to stop.

That's right. And then later in the day it might be quiet for a long time, and she was gone. I'd say her name and it was as if she didn't even hear me. What was that like?

Like being a ghost.

See? You're not so bad at this. All you have to do is give a shit and think for a moment. This was my real life, not a story. These were days I lived, as real as your days now. And tell me about my friends. Who did I see? Who were my friends and family for those years?

No one.

And who made sure I got to have my childhood? Who made sure I went to school and had decent clothes and went to birthday parties and finished my homework?

No one.

No one. And who is my father now?

My grandpa.

I expected her to hit me, but she didn't. She let go of my arms and retreated back across the seat to her place behind the wheel. She put on her seat belt and pulled out carefully into the slow lane and drove without speaking to me. Sound of the wipers, sound of wet roads, slush thrown by the wake of trucks as they passed, covering our windshield, blotting out everything and then clear again. Our turnoff to the industrial section, almost no one else living here, narrow strip of houses and apartments between an airfield and parking lots.

We walked upstairs, and at the door my mother stopped. I'm going to give you one last chance, she said. Over the next day or two, you'll live what I lived then, and that will be your chance to see.

What does that mean?

That's what you'll be learning.

My mother dropped all her clothes just inside our door, in the kitchen. She stripped naked. Cold white with splotches of red on her back. A strong back, and she let out her ponytail and sat down on the cold tiles of the floor.

It's all you, she said. Run me a bath, and then drag me over and get me on the toilet seat and then in the tub. Then fix dinner, but don't forget to check on me in case I might be drowning or dying in some other way.

What?

You heard me. Start working. It's going to be a long night for you, and then a long day, and then a long night, and after a while, you won't care whether it's day or night. You'll only want to sleep.

My mother lay down on the floor. I'm getting cold, she said. Better hurry with that bath. And don't let my skin rub when you drag me. She always said it felt like her skin could rip off. I always had to be so careful with her skin.

I hurried to the bathroom, put in the drain plug and ran the water, not too hot. I didn't believe this game would go on long. I would put her in the bath and fix dinner, and then we'd watch TV and I could go to bed.

I grabbed her wrists to drag, but she had gone limp, head lolling, and was so heavy and stuck to the floor.

I pulled again and she screamed and I dropped her wrists, which slapped hard against the tiles.

She screamed if I pulled like that, my mother said. You can't yank anything, or rub anything. Cancer spreads everywhere. It might begin in one place, but it travels inside and new places become sore. You never know what part of her might hurt next. I used to think if I pulled an arm too hard it might come off, rotten at the joint. All her joints were sore, and bruises everywhere.

I can't do this.

My mother smiled. That's right. That's what I said, though not so early. You're being a baby. You don't get to say I can't do this until a few months have gone by. That's when you say it and mean it.

I took one of the towels from the bathroom and laid it on the floor beside her. How do I get you on the towel?

There were no instructions, my mother said. No one ever told me how to do anything.

I knelt on the floor and tried to push the towel in along her back, lifted her shoulder blade with one hand. But I wasn't strong enough from this angle. I had to kneel on the other side and lean over and pull her toward me, my face in close to her armpit, strong smell of sweat from a day of work. Skin clammy and not soft like Shalini's. My naked mother. I held her close and pulled the towel under, then moved down lower to her hips, all the dark hair down there, and rolled her toward me. She was so much bigger than I was, stronger and taller.

I crossed her arms over her chest, knelt in close behind her head, and pulled on the towel beneath to slide her along the floor. She could have been a dead body. We hit carpet and stopped. I pulled and could not drag her. I can't do this, I said.

You will. You will or you no longer have a mother. I will leave, just leave, like my father did, and you will never hear from me again.

My eyes wet as soon as she said that, and I hated being such a baby. I pulled harder and dragged her across the carpet down the small hallway to the bathroom tile, where she slid easily again.

The water in the tub was already too high, so I turned it off. I struggled to lift her onto the toilet seat. Sideways a bit, and she was not helping, just limp, but finally she was settled there and peed while I waited. Smell of her pee thick in the air, sound of the tub overflow drain sucking.

Wipe me, she said, so I wrapped toilet paper on my hand and reached between her legs to wipe. Something I could never have imagined doing.

Now the tub.

I put my arms around and locked my hands and dragged. I eased her carefully into the water, her feet at the faucet end. She was so tall her knees were bent.

Now bathe me, and don't forget dinner.

Which do I do first?

Both at the same time. Everything always at the same time.

I'll be right back, I said. I went to the kitchen and put a pot of water on the stove to boil, found a box of pasta. No spaghetti sauce in the fridge or cupboard, but I knew she'd tell me I had to figure it out myself, so I found a can of tomato soup, and there were some mushrooms I could add.

I hurried back to the tub and grabbed a bar of soap.

You have to wash my hair, too.

I looked at her long hair, and how tall she was in the tub. I went back to the kitchen for a small pot.

Lean forward, I said, and I scooped bathwater in the pot and poured it carefully over her head.

That's right, she said. I'm too hot, though. I can't breathe, Sheri. That's what she'd say. I can't breathe.

I ran the cold tap and swirled the water around.

There's no air in here.

I looked around. We didn't have a bathroom window or fan. There was never any way to air out the bathroom.

Air! she yelled. I need air! I'm dying!

I ran out and opened our front door and living room window, let the icy air billow in low. Like steam pouring over the windowsill, as if temperature had been reversed. The air we breathed really a liquid, but we saw it only in rare moments like this. Fog born suddenly from nothing, flooding from nowhere, no fog bank outside, no ocean or mountains at the edge. And it wasn't summer. Fog was usually in summer.

Sheri! she yelled.

When I ran back to the tub, she slapped me. I could have died. I could have drowned. Leaving me like that, with my head bent forward into the water. Do you want to kill me? And I'm cold now. It's freezing in here.

I opened the hot water tap and hurried out to the door and window, clouds forming at the margins and then gone. They rushed in and vanished somehow. I closed the gates to them, cut them off, and my mother yelled again.

I'm burning! You stupid little shit. Goddamn it, Sheri. You left the hot water on.

I panicked and went for the hot water tap, turned it off, and then swirled the water around with my hand.

My feet are burned.

Even her voice was different, my mother gone. I could not believe my grandmother had been this way, cruel and bitter.

Please, I said. I understand. We can stop.

You don't understand anything yet. You don't believe. You're not going to school tomorrow, and I'm not going to work. Where's my dinner, Sheri?

Don't call me Sheri.

My mother grabbed my hair and shoved my face down into the tub water. It was so fast I hadn't taken a breath. I had no air, panicking. I couldn't pull my head up. She was so strong. I fought. I punched at her and yanked my whole body, but she had the weight of oceans, pressing down, and then she released me.

You will hate me, she said. I know you will hate me. But my mother did all of these things and I loved her. And I am going to make you see. You will know what it was like, and that's all I care about.

I don't care about your stupid life! I screamed.

That's the problem. We're going to end that. Now fix dinner.

I was gasping and dripping, and I wanted to run, just run away. She did not even look like my mother, not caring at all that I was hurt. She looked at me coldly, as if I were a stranger.

Fix my dinner, Sheri.

So I did it. I put the pasta in the water that was at a full boil. It looked like rage, bubbles forming sourceless and ripped away and burst. Perfect form of rage. The yellow dried pasta sinking in and calming. I punctured the tomato soup with the can opener when my mother called out again.

Get me out of this bath, Sheri!

She was angry I hadn't made her clean. You know I can't be in the water for long. I'll get sick. I can't breathe. But I'm still filthy.

I knelt beside her with the bar of soap and tried to wash her, but soap doesn't work underwater. It feels too rough, doesn't slide or lather.

Don't tear my skin off, she said.

I ran the soap along her belly and breasts and thighs and followed with my other hand, my chest braced on the edge of the tub. I washed between her legs, tried to reach under along her back, reaching down beneath the surface into a distortion of texture and size and shape, my mother become only a body and not even that, more rubbery than that.

Stop, she said. You have to get me out of here.

I could hear the pasta scum boiling over onto the burner, but I had to lift her from the tub, dead weight. Water all over the floor, and I was afraid of slipping. I couldn't hold her up, so I sat her down on the tile leaning back against the tub.

No! she yelled. I'm freezing. This floor and the outside of the tub. Do you want me to die?

I don't know where to put you.

Don't whine. Move me onto the bed and dry me there.

So I dragged her down the hall.

My heels are dragging against the carpet. Pick me up.

I can't.

Pick me up.

I couldn't answer. I kept dragging until I could ease her onto the bed.

Don't get my bed wet.

I ran back for a towel, tried to be quick but gentle, dried her hair first.

I'm cold, and I'm hungry. You were a mistake, Sheri. If it hadn't been for you, none of this would have happened.

What?

After the pregnancy, everything changed. My chemistry, how I'm made. I smelled different, my skin dried out, my hair. I couldn't even eat the things I ate before. I was allergic for the first time. You changed everything inside me, an invasion, and that has to be when the cancer started. It's because of you that I'm dying.

That's not fair.

That's what I said.

She wouldn't have said those things.

But she did, and after a while I believed them, because I was fourteen and there was no one else and she kept saying them, and I was watching her dying. I believed that I brought the cancer into her, that I was an infection.

But that's not possible, is it?

Anything is possible with a parent. Parents are gods. They make us and they destroy us. They warp the world and remake it in their own shape, and that's the world we know forever after. It's the only world. We can't see what it might have looked like otherwise.

I'm sorry.

You're not done yet. Don't think you're done. You've only just started. Where's my dinner?

I had forgotten the pasta. I ran for the pot. Most of the water was gone, the spaghetti clumped and not fully covered, but I drained the small bit of water into the sink.

Sheri! she yelled. I'm freezing!

I rushed back to her, and she was so angry, screaming at me. You left me wet! Out in the cold air! You're a worthless little bitch. I should have killed you.

I was drying her with the towel, as quickly and carefully as I could, but I was crying, my eyes filled entirely and blinking and I couldn't see well. My grandmother could not have been so cruel.

Get me under the covers.

So I finished drying her and pulled away the comforter and sheet from the other side of the bed and rolled her gently into place, and that's when we heard the neighbors bang on the wall, protesting my mother's screaming.

She charged out of bed, the sick made suddenly well, as if miracles could be performed, and she banged the wall with her fist. Fuck off! she yelled.

They yelled, she yelled, banging from both sides, my mother standing there naked and hair wet, arms raised and shouting to a white wall, and then she was back, lying down, yanking the comforter and sheet into place. Well, she said. You'll have to do a better job or it's going to be a long night for them too.

I'll finish dinner.

That's right.

I poured the can of tomato soup directly into the drained pot of spaghetti and put it back on the burner. I stirred and tried to break apart the clumps. I added some pepper and grabbed two plates and hurried back with our meal.

Sheri, my mother said when I returned. My good little girl. You're an angel, you know that?

I didn't know what to say. I gave her a plate and fork.

I'm not hungry, she said. I can't eat. Just come and lie down next to me.

So I set the plates on the floor and lay down beside my mother and she put an arm around me, her other hand stroking my hair. I was so tense I was grinding my teeth. I expected her to twist my neck or pull my hair.

Sheri, you're an angel. I made you. I made you perfect. This body died to make you.

She played with my hair and began humming to herself, some simple song I didn't recognize. You have to remember me, she said. When I'm gone, you're the only one to keep my memory alive. So you have to understand. Sometimes I say things because I have unbearable pain, but that's not me. That's not who I am. Do you understand?

Yes.

That's good, Sheri. That's good. I don't need to be forgiven, because I've done nothing wrong. If you do something out of pain, it can never be a crime.

She kissed the back of my head and then stayed there, her mouth in my hair. Pain offers only one choice, Sheri. You have to run from it. You have to try to escape. There's no other choice, because it's more terrible than anything else. People complain about emotional pain or psychological pain, the pain of loss, but this is nothing compared to pure physical agony. You'll twist and turn until you rip yourself apart. You'll scream and destroy and fight everything and everyone if it brings even a single moment in which you're not as fully aware of the pain. You have to understand this, or you'll think I'm a monster.

But you don't have this pain, I said. Your mother had this pain.

You can't do it, can you? You can't be generous and try to imagine another life, even your mother's. You can't be Sheri for one night and try to understand what it was like for me to be left alone with my dying mother. Do you think it made the cruelty any better to hear that it wasn't her fault? She still screamed and slapped me and did horrible things. She still took away my childhood and also my future. Was there a bigger price I could have paid? My childhood and my adulthood.

I didn't make you pay.

My mother's arms wrapped around my head, and I really thought she might twist and break my neck. True, she said. That's true. And what have I always told you? Not to ever let me blame you for my problems. I didn't talk about the past. I've done everything to protect you, so you wouldn't have to go through what I did. And how have you thanked me for that?

I haven't done anything.

But you have. You won't rest until the three of us are skipping hand in hand.

We could live at his house, and he could take me to school. You wouldn't have to work as much.

Maybe your brain just isn't old enough. He committed a crime. He's responsible for that. He doesn't get to have everything given to him as if he never did anything wrong. Nineteen years. I didn't see him for nineteen years.

Then why miss the years now?

My mother rolled away from me on the bed. You're smart, Caitlin. You're hard to argue with. But he is no longer my father. He gave up that right. And I will not let him be a grandfather, because really I want to see him burn. I want to set a match to him and watch him scream. I want him to feel unbearable pain. I want him to feel more pain than there is in this world. There's not enough pain available for him.

I woke in darkness, my arm shaken.

Take me to the bathroom, Sheri.

What? I didn't remember at first, disoriented.

Take me now or the sheets will need changing. And actually, you should experience that.

Experience what?

I could smell her piss then, acidic and thick.

Oops, she said.

I yanked the comforter and top sheet back. What are you doing?

Change the sheets, Sheri. And clean me. How could you let this happen?

You did this. You wet the bed.

Letting your own mother die in her bed pissing herself. Do you hate me so much?

I got up and turned on the light. My mother naked on the bed with a yellowish spot on the sheet, spreading. I'm cold, Sheri. Curling as if she were weak.

You're not sick. You're not your mother. I'm not Sheri.

I'm cold, Sheri. And if you don't take care of me, I will leave. Maybe you don't believe that. But it's true. I will leave. You will understand your mother and care about her life or you don't deserve to have a mother.

She looked the same as my mother from before. Nothing had changed, except that nothing made sense now. Lying in her own urine.

I'm cold, Sheri! she screamed. I looked at her bedside clock, and it was after three a.m. I'll get a towel, I said, and I ran to the bathroom, grabbed a small towel and soaked it in warm water, wrung it out.

I grabbed her legs carefully at the knees and pulled her to the side, away from the spot. And then I wiped her with the warm wet towel, wiped everywhere carefully, all the way to her lower back and down her thighs.

I'm cold!

I arranged the top sheet carefully over her, not letting it touch the urine, and then I arranged the comforter. Then it was time to strip the sheet from under her.

I started at the head of the bed, pulled off the corners and lifted her gently.

You're hurting me, she said.

I'm doing my best.

This isn't about you.

I kept pulling that sheet and lifting each part of her body, as if I were a priestess and she were some god made of flesh. No prayers or sacrifice except caring for the body, and all must be kept quiet. All our movements meant only not to anger. You had to do everything perfectly, I said. And she was still angry.

Yes. That's right. You're learning.

You were afraid the whole time.

Yes. But not afraid of her yelling at me or slapping me or any of that. What was I afraid of?

That she would die.

And what else?

That it would be your fault.

Yes.

My mother sat up then, and she hugged me. This is good, Caitlin. You're good. I think you really understand something of what it was like.

But he's still my grandpa, and I get to see him.

My mother let go of me and lay back down. Clean that spot. Use a little bit of bleach and water. Then dry it with a hair dryer. And let me sleep, Sheri. Why can't you let me sleep? I'm tired.

I did what you wanted. I understood your life.

My mother smiled. Yeah. You understand everything. Let's talk again tomorrow night, in another twenty-four hours, after you've worked and had almost no sleep. You haven't been broken yet. I'm going to break you, and then we'll find out who you are.

I pulled the rest of the sheet free and bunched it up and

carried it to the washer. I didn't turn it on because of the neighbors. Then I found the bottle of bleach and poured a little bit in a bucket with some warm water and grabbed a sponge.

The mattress had other stains, old. And it seemed it might soak up a lot of water, so I was sparing. I wondered whether my grandfather was awake, too. Where was his house, and what was it like? I was almost like Cinderella dreaming of the prince, except he was an old man, not a prince, and his house would be small, no castle, and this was my real mother, not my stepmother, and she had already destroyed the carriage. But the idea was the same, to leave the old life and have a new and better one.

I'm Cinderella, I said. You were Cinderella.

No I wasn't.

You had to work. You didn't get to have your life. You had to take care of someone else.

That's true. But there was no prince waiting, no one to take me away. You don't see me in a castle now, do you?

What about a house, and not having to work? What if I could get him to agree that you don't have to work anymore? He could be a mechanic again. He would do that. I know he would. And you can spend time with Steve as your prince.

It's a fairy tale, Caitlin. That means it's not real. There's a real life and there's a fantasy life.

And Cinderella gets to have the fantasy. That becomes her real life.

Yeah. You're right. But that doesn't happen for us. We don't get to cross over. Whatever road you're on, that goes all the way to the grave.

I put the bucket down on the floor, and I didn't know how to convince her. I sniffed the spot on the mattress, and it was mostly bleach now. I couldn't tell whether the urine was still there or not.

I used the hair dryer on low to not disturb the neighbors. This gentle hot wind drying the urine spot, such a strange thing in the middle of the night. I was so exhausted my eyes kept closing.

What if you could go back to school? I asked. If you can't just be given a new life, how about the chance to make a new life? He would work, and we'd live at his house, and you would go to school.

It's not the same. I'd be about fifteen years late, too old. And where's his punishment? It's not enough that he has to work again. He needs to die alone. You're forgetting that part.

You're just mean.

Yes. Yes I am. But I want to be a thousand times meaner. I can't possibly say anything bad enough. I'd have to pull my guts out through my mouth to be saying enough. And maybe not even then. You have a goodness, a generosity, and I don't want you to lose that. But I lost it almost twenty years ago.

I felt the spot with my hand. The mattress hot now, and only barely damp. It seemed fine. So I went to the closet for a new fitted sheet and did my side of the bed first, pulled the sheet all the way over and then rolled her gently and attached her side. All better, I said, but she didn't answer.

I noticed then that both our dinner plates were empty on the floor beside her. She had eaten both dinners while I was sleeping, and I was starving now. So I went to the kitchen and fixed a bowl of cereal. Almost four a.m. on the kitchen clock. At least we weren't going to work and school and I could sleep in. Sound only of the refrigerator, and light only from the hallway. I sat in shadow in a quiet world waiting.

When I returned to bed, she spoke. I need medicine. You have to go out now.

Streetlamps hunched over, softened cones of light and dark spaces between. I hurried along the sidewalk, my chin and hands buried. The cold a dull ache already in my legs. I could almost feel my bones.

I thought there would be no other movement, no one else awake, but a white van passed, and then another, and a car coming the other way. For Boeing Field, maybe, everything starting so early.

I didn't know where I would find a store open. I was looking for a 7-Eleven or a gas station. She wanted a painkiller and something to keep her from throwing up. She said she had made these night trips all the time.

Corson Avenue South had become part of a field of white indistinguishable from sidewalks and front yards and the parking lots except that it was bordered by these lights and had slim dark tracks from the few cars. I crossed over on South Harney Street to get to Airport Way South, thinking there had to be some stores or gas stations, but there were only windowless warehouses, small office complexes, a few cafes closed. A bakery, and even that wasn't open yet. Interstate 5 a corridor of light, trucks arriving early in the city, come from anywhere.

For some reason, I didn't feel afraid. Perhaps because of the snow. When I hit Corson again, at the top of Airport Way, an overpass rose above like a landing strip. Old trucks, rusted and dented, and wrecked cars on the other side of the street, kept for parts. The street no longer lit under the overpass, forming a kind of cave, but I walked along the mouth of this cave and met no one. A park, then, behind chain-link fence, and I just kept going on Corson back toward our apartment, and then I saw someone walking toward me, another figure hunched over and bundled up and pushing through the snow, rushing now, and I stopped, confused, not knowing whether to run, but my mother called out, Caitlin!

I stood in place. I didn't run to her. In fact, I looked back behind me, at that cave of an overpass, some instinct for escape. The weight of her, momentum, snow flung by each plow of her boots. Some shadow figure from fairy tale, come to rescue or destroy. As if we lived in the woods, no concrete beneath the white, that overpass the curve of a mountain, faced in cliffs. Each warehouse a dark grove with fields between, small clearings. And I was not fast enough. I couldn't move. In fairy tale, you can never get away.

She caught me, pulled me tight against her. Caitlin, she said. My baby. I'm sorry. Kissing my forehead and cradling me. You can't be out here.

Wolves, she might have said. But there were no wolves.

I used to walk along the highway, she said. Day or night, alone. I can't even think of it. It makes me crazy. Don't ever come out here again. You understand?

Yes, I said.

There are men out here. Always men. They will rape you. They will rape both of us, if they find us now. We have to get back.

So she grabbed my hand and we ran through the snow together, as if a pack of men ran just behind at our heels. We exploded up the stairs and my mother fumbled with the keys at the lock and then we were inside, safe.

Everything bad in this world comes from men, my mother said. You have to know that. All violence, all fear, all slavery. Everything that crushes us.

We sat on the kitchen floor, with our backs against the door to barricade. The lights out, so we wouldn't be seen.

I'm sorry, she said. I went too far. Don't ever tell anyone I sent you out in the snow. At night, in this place. And don't tell anyone I dunked your head underwater. You can't tell anyone that.

I won't, I said. And I thought, who would I tell? Only my grandpa or Shalini, and I wouldn't tell my grandpa, because I wanted him to like her. I wanted them to get along. So only Shalini, and when would I see her again? I missed her suddenly with this deep and hollow ache in my chest. I wanted her to lie on top of me. I wanted to kiss her and feel her skin against mine. And I wanted to be able to tell my mother.

I miss Shalini.

Well you're not going to school today.

But today's Friday. That means I won't see her until Monday.

Don't whine. You need to get me in bed and catch some sleep if you can. You still have a lot of work ahead of you.

Shalini is the best friend I've ever had. Not like other friends.

I don't care about Shalini. By this time next year, you'll have forgotten all about her. Or it could be next week. Focus. You're Sheri now. You're going to learn what exhaustion is, and despair.

I'll never forget Shalini.

Yeah, whatever. You're twelve. Everything is so important in your life right now. Real life-and-death stuff, the world holding its breath. Now drag me to bed.

I was so angry, but she had the power to make me never see Shalini again and never see my grandfather again. She had the power to do anything. She could have decided we were moving to some other part of the country. Or she could have just vanished forever. So I hunched over and pulled her to the bedroom.

I'm not due at work until Monday morning, she said. All of today and then three more nights. That's how long it could be. You might want to become a faster learner.

No Shalini, no school, no aquarium, no Grandpa. All taken away. My back had tightened up, stiff as I dragged. And then we were at the bedside and I hauled her off the ground and we fell onto the mattress.

Sleep, she said. Sleep while you can. Forget where you are and forget the mountain of days. Each one enormous, lost in some forest that never ends, but then the edge will fold back and you'll walk on what was the sky and is now only another forest floor, another layer, and you can feel the weight of hundreds of these layers above you. Like an ant climbing tunnel after tunnel in darkness and the mountain never ends. Think of that. More than a thousand days, each one never ending.

My mother facedown in her pillow, yawning now, falling into sleep. She had never left that mountain of days. Her mother had died, but that hadn't been the end of the forest. I wanted more than anything to free her.

Sheri. I was confused at first, but then I knew my mother was calling me. Sheri. I struggled awake and could smell urine again, and more. The awful, overpowering smell of shit right here in the bed with us.

Ah! I gasped. I thought I might vomit.

Clean me up, Sheri. Letting your mother die in her own shit, like an animal.

Stop this!

I wish I could. I wish I could stop dying, believe me. I wish you could die instead. The cancer came from you.

You're crazy! I screamed. I was out of the bed already, running out of the room.

You will come back here and clean this.

I opened the front door and went outside in my underwear. Still snowing. Everything blanketed, only the sides of buildings showing, and thin tracks in the road. The piles of traffic barriers still orange. I gulped in the fresh, cold air and my bare feet ached already. I could run, just run to every neighbor and see if anyone would take me in.

Sheri! I don't want to smell this. This is vile. What have you done?

My skin tightening, all heat already gone. My body thin and pale, flushing pink. It seemed a long way down to my feet. A body such an unlikely thing, the shape of it and how fragile it was, exposed.

I marched into the bathroom and wrapped each hand in toilet paper, then I went to my mother and pulled back the top sheet. She had rolled over onto it, mashed all against her backside. My mouth opened to retch, but I held it back. I grabbed two handfuls with my toilet paper mitts, wiping, and carried them to the toilet, flushed, and wrapped again.

I tried not to touch, but I had to get in between her legs, and there was the angle with the sheet, and the toilet paper too thin.

Don't be so rough, my mother said. You're hurting me.

So I tried to be gentle as I wiped the backs of her thighs and butt and crotch and the sheet, and nothing was clean, and the smell was no less.

Baby wipes, my mother said. Baby wipes and then baby powder. You need to buy those things or my skin will get a rash.

I couldn't answer. I was still trying not to throw up, keeping my mouth closed. I grabbed a small hand towel and soaked it in warm water, then wrung it out. I wiped her with this and she complained.

It hurts. Damn it, Sheri. You're tearing off my skin.

But I ignored her, washed out the towel at the sink, unbelievably nasty, something I never thought I'd have to see, all over my bare hands, and then returned to wipe again until she was clean. I pulled off the corners of the sheet, rolled her gently to the side, and wrapped it in a ball.

You do this a hundred times, she said. Imagine that. A hundred times, no less. The shit soaks into the mattress. You can't get the smell out. You use bleach and soap and shampoo, and you even try gasoline once. There are two beds, so at first you just flip her mattress. Then you use both sides of yours. But that's only the beginning. It happens so many more times. If you had money, you could buy adult diapers, but you don't have any money. So you try making diapers from towels, but there's no elastic, so it all spills out the sides. Almost always diarrhea. A brown lumpy drool with bits of red in it, sometimes blood. And the smell is sulfur. Not like my shit now. This is nothing. This is healthy. But when someone is sick, that sulfur smell, the smell of gunpowder or rotten eggs, that smell is everywhere, and that's what soaked into the mattresses, the smell of sickness and death.

I'm sorry, I said.

Just understand. I slept in that smell for years, but my bed should have been kept separate. I should have been kept safe. That's what he didn't do, keep me safe. I don't know how to say it any more clearly.

I understand. And he should have been there. He shouldn't have left.

Good, Caitlin. Good.

There's nothing he can ever do to make it up to you.

Yes. That's right.

You suffered something no one should have to suffer.

Yes.

And you lost everything, and it can't be returned, and your life will never be what it should have been.

My mother sat up. Caitlin. I'm proud of you. That's good.

And she died without her husband. He committed a crime.

Yes.

And he can never make that better for her, because she's gone.

Yes.

He's a monster. He's unforgivable. He should be hated. He should have nothing, and he should die alone.

Caitlin. Yes. My mother looked excited, as if we had discovered something, as if we were going on an adventure.

But he's still my grandpa.

My mother slumped back down into her pillow. I stood and waited, but she said nothing. Aren't you going to scream at me? I asked.

Gray light of day in the room. My mother's back almost the same color as the white mattress, lying in her bed nineteen years ago, when she was me. I waited.

The clock said almost one p.m. I'll fix lunch, I said.

I dumped the sheets in the washer with the others and used all the highest settings, poured in bleach as well as detergent. It would be a shitshake, and I'd have to wash a couple more times, I was sure. I mixed a bucket of bleach and water and took another small towel and wiped at the spot on the bed while my mother remained silent. I didn't sniff-test the mattress when I was done. And I could smell my mother. She wasn't quite clean.

I'll run you a bath.

No response, but I went to the tub and was careful to get the temperature right. I poured in some shampoo.

In the kitchen, I looked for something fast, found cans of chili. I could fight her. I knew I was strong enough. I could last until Monday morning. I opened both cans and shook them into the pot, put it on low.

I checked on her, but she hadn't moved. Eyes open, not sleeping, but not responding.

When the bath was ready, I rolled her over to face the middle of the bare mattress, got behind to hug and pull. Already, in less than a day, we had pathways repeated over and over. A thousand days did seem terrifying. I didn't want to know what her life had been like then.

I eased her into the tub, arranged her limp legs and arms and head, and she stared down into the water but didn't look like she could fall.

The chili was warm, and I brought her a bowl. She didn't raise her arms. So I fed her spoonful by spoonful and she moved her mouth just enough to open and chew, some zombie come partially to life. Normally she would have been at work right now, in the snow and lights, an outpost of clanking metal and revving diesel engines run nonstop day and night all year. A place where she was no longer herself but only a body performing tasks, a kind of robot that looked like a person. But now she was the opposite, dead on the outside and lost somewhere inside what could only be her, remembering.

When she finished her bowl, I went out to the kitchen to eat. I was trying to see my grandmother. We had no photos. My mother had erased everything. The silence in the house, no speaking for days. I saw her older. I couldn't see her my own mother's age. Wrinkled face, and I couldn't make her cruel, only sad. She would smile to say she was sorry about dying, sorry to leave and not be there for all that would happen in later years, sorry for all that was being taken away. This was the only grandmother I could imagine, sorrowing and still filled with love.

The bathwater had already lost its heat, so quickly, and she was sitting in it, probably getting chilled now, but not saying anything. It was worse than when she yelled at me.

I have to get you out of here, I said. I'm sorry. I had meant to soap her more carefully, but the soak in shampoo suds would have to be enough.

I tugged but she was entirely limp, so heavy. I couldn't dry her off but dragged her dripping back to the bed made with our last clean sheets, laid her on my side and toweled her off, crotch last, a few small brown smears, then rolled her over and tucked her in with a top sheet and comforter.

You're clean now, I said, and warm. Just sleep.

She closed her eyes and said nothing.

When I lifted the lid of the washer and sniffed, the sheets seemed clean. I smelled only laundry detergent, but I poured in more, with bleach again, added the towel, and washed a second time. Then draining the bathtub and rinsing it, wiping up the floor. Then dishes.

I was so exhausted. I went to my own bed, not wanting to wake up ever again next to shit or piss, and I must have fallen asleep instantly, then woke to knocking.

I looked at my bedside clock and it was already six thirty in the evening, dark out, the day gone and someone knocking at our door.

My mother wasn't answering. I struggled to wake up, pulled myself out of bed to go check on her. She was lying on her side just as I'd left her, unmoved, her eyes open now.

Should I answer? I asked.

No response from her, so I went to the door. Who is it?

Steve.

The sound of his voice the most enormous relief. He could break the spell.

Where's your mom? he asked when I let him in. He looked like a normal person, friendly, talking, not pretending to be someone else, dressed and clean, not pissing himself. He was carrying a bag of groceries and a rose.

In bed.

In bed? Can I see her?

I pointed to her room and he set the bag on the kitchen counter, then went to her. I followed.

It smells in here, he said. Like shit. What happened?

My mother hadn't moved. Leave, she said. Caitlin and I are spending the weekend together.

You weren't at work today, he said. I went by at lunch, and they said you called in sick.

Just leave.

Not so easy. I decided I'm not leaving, that I won't let you drive me out. Because I know you want me to stay.

Caitlin, my mother said. I need to pee.

I dragged her naked from the bed toward the toilet.

What's going on? Steve said. What happened? Can't you walk? His voice so quiet it was only air. He was afraid.

She's fine, I said, struggling to talk as I dragged her. She's just showing me what it was like to take care of her mother.

What?

Caitlin doesn't believe my life was real. She wants her happy grandpa time, and she doesn't believe any of what happened when he left. So I'm showing her.

That's crazy. And you're naked.

Get the fuck out.

Not this time.

I had my mother on the toilet seat finally. She peed as Steve watched from the doorway.

What? she said. Years of taking care of her. No one will ever know what that was like, but knowing a few days can't hurt.

How long has this been going on?

Since yesterday, I said. In the evening. After she destroyed his car with the tire iron.

You saw your father?

You should hear the plans, she said. They're making plans

now. We're supposed to move in with him, a happy little family. Our sugar daddy, saving Cinderella. He goes back to work as a mechanic, watches fish with Caitlin, and I go back to school and skip around meadows with all my free time. You get to be the prince. Caitlin has it all planned out.

What?

I know he would work again, I said. And he already told us we could live with him and not pay rent. And she could go back to school.

That's a lot to think about, Steve said.

I'm not thinking about it, my mother said.

Well why not? You hate your job, and I know you could do something better if you had a chance. Maybe you should at least consider it.

Wipe me.

I wiped my mother and then grabbed her from behind again.

Stop it! Steve yelled. What the fuck are you doing?

Oh, so upsetting, having to drag a healthy person to bed. Try someone whose body is turning to rot.

Steve followed us into the bedroom. Why does it smell so bad in here?

It's not the right smell. It really was sulfur, day and night, as if the bowels of the earth were breaking open, as if we lived in hell. When I hear fire and brimstone, that's what I think of, my mother's bedroom. And always some new wicked torment from her, saying something crazy, how I had made her sick or driven everyone away or didn't love her.

I pulled my mother onto the bed and rolled her over, covered her with the sheet and comforter.

Now leave me alone. Make dinner, Sheri.

You're calling her Sheri?

Yep. I'm trying to break into that selfish little skull.

Caitlin isn't selfish.

She's a child. All children are selfish. And what would you know? You've never raised a kid. So I'll tell you. We aren't real. We don't have any feelings or thoughts that aren't about her. She can't believe we existed before her. So I'm making her live that time. It will become a part of her own memories, and then she'll believe.

That's crazy.

You call me crazy one more time and I will cut you open with a knife.

Look, I'm sorry. But please stop. Why can't you just stop?

Because I didn't get to be selfish.

Steve knelt beside my mother where she curled in bed, put his arm over her. Sheri, he said. I love you, and I won't leave you. And Caitlin will always love you more than anyone else. She watches you in every moment, and whatever you're feeling in that moment determines whether the world is good or about to end. She's your daughter.

He laid his head against hers, arms wrapped around, and I could see her convulse beneath the sheet, short quick tugs from crying, but no sound. I ran to her and put my arms around also.

Sheri, he said. Things could be easier for you now. Let them be easier.

But I hate him so much.

Maybe it's because you love him. Something left over.

You're a bastard.

That's right. I'll be whatever you need me to be.

Mom, I said. I'm sorry.

I could feel my mother convulse again, soundless. I held her as tightly as I could.

You're sorry, she finally said. After how awful I've been to you. Well, I guess that decides it. Fuck. I can't believe that piece of shit gets to have his way again. It's not fair.

Steve made clam chowder with razor clams from Alaska. As big as his hands, brown shells brittle and sharp. I froze these last summer when I was in a hurry, he said. You dig after them with a shovel. At low tide. The sand is black. Then you're on your knees or even lying down on the wet beach as you dig in with your hand, sometimes all the way to your shoulder. They're unbelievably fast, and you're grabbing at this hose which is their mouth and butt, called a siphon, but sometimes you grab the shell and it shatters and that's how you get cut.

The siphon on each clam long and dirty cream. Steve wedged a shell apart, pulled out the meat, cleaned the stomach, rinsed, and then chopped the clam into small bits.

How do you know where to dig?

They leave a sign in the sand. Called a keyhole if it's clear or a dimple if it's already filled in, or even a doughnut if you can see sand humped up all around the hole.

And why do they have their mouths next to their butts?

Seems like a bad choice. I'd hate to wake up one day and find my butt next to my mouth.

I laughed and hit Steve in the arm. She was taking a shower after cleaning her room, so he was all mine at the moment.

See how the shells look like trees? Steve said.

What?

Like a cross-section, if you cut a tree trunk. They have rings, and those really are growth rings, just like on a tree.

Do the trees know about this?

Steve laughed. That could mean trouble for the clams. You're right.

My mother emerged, her hair wet, wearing a long flannel shirt and no pants.

Whoa, Steve said. I like that look.

The shirt was held together by only one button, very low. My mother moving in for the kill. Come here, she said. Dinner will have to wait.

So I was left alone in the kitchen thinking of Shalini, this unbearable feeling of wanting to pull at the air. I wouldn't see her until Monday, and it was only Friday night. I found her mother's phone number and dialed.

Shalini's father answered. This is late to be calling, he said. But I'll allow it this once.

I miss you, I whispered when she came on the line.

Why weren't you at school?

I wanted to explain to her, but it was all too enormous. I didn't know where to begin. I don't know, I said.

You don't know?

Just call me back now and invite me for a sleepover tomorrow. We won't tell my mother I called first.

Okay, but your family is very strange.

Yes.

I hung up the phone then, quietly, and waited. I could hear my mother and Steve having sex. I wanted to know what it was like, what they were doing. I tried to imagine it and couldn't imagine anything. They sounded so desperate. I could only remember the feel of Shalini's skin, her heat and breath.

The phone rang and I jumped, startled.

You are cordially invited to the Anand residence, Shalini said, then laughed. We await the pleasure of your company.

Yes, I said, loud enough for my mother to hear. Thank you. I'll see you tomorrow.

You sound like a robot.

Yes, we remember where. Thank you.

You're so weird. My mother says you can come after lunch again, but we have to sleep this time. I was so tired last time.

You're not going to sleep, I whispered. Not even five minutes.

Shalini laughed.

I sat in the kitchen alone afterward, still waiting, and felt hot and jittery, as if Shalini were right here. I wanted her in my mouth, some instinct to devour. I would swallow her whole and keep her inside. My hands were tingling and my legs felt weak. I could hardly breathe.

The moaning had stopped from my mother's room, and soon they reappeared, my mother wearing jeans this time, her shirt buttoned. I wanted to ask, What did you do?

Who was that on the phone? my mother asked.

Shalini. She invited me for a sleepover tomorrow. Can I go? Please?

My mother smiled. Sure. And I'm sorry about what I said, sweet pea. I'm sure she is important and that you will remember her.

I could never forget her.

My mother kissed me on the forehead and then sat on a kitchen stool next to Steve. She smelled like him.

Steve wasn't dicing the last clams. He spread them out wet and glistening on the cutting board, then dipped in egg and rolled in bread crumbs. Clam fritters, he said. Horse ovaries, before the chowder.

Horse ovaries? I asked.

Fancy French term for appetizers. He winked at me. This is hot culture you're getting here.

My mother laughed.

He melted butter in our largest frying pan and laid in the breaded clams. Then he returned to the chowder. He was cooking onions and garlic in butter at the bottom of our largest pot. There are three secrets in every restaurant, he said. Do you know what they are? He lifted his eyebrows at me.

I don't know.

You're not trying.

I know, my mother said. The higher the price, the less food you get.

True, Steve said. True. But three secrets for every restaurant, cheap or expensive.

The food is from yesterday? I asked.

Butter, Steve said. Butter is secret number one. Then salt and sugar. Anything you order will have butter, and you'll think it's rich and worth the money you're paying. Salt makes you taste it and want more. Sugar makes you think it's subtle, that there are other flavors here. But even cardboard would taste good in butter, salt, and sugar. The three food groups.

Well, my mother said. That's my last time going to a restaurant.

As if we ever go to restaurants, I said.

Watch it. And why can't we go to restaurants now? This is when the fairy tale begins. Remember?

Steve was ignoring us, tossing the diced clams into the pot, handful after handful.

Well? my mother asked. Don't I get to go to restaurants now?

Yes, I said. He'll take us to restaurants.

But you don't know, do you? There's not really any deal. We're acting like there's a deal, but nothing has been agreed.

He'll say yes.

But yes to what? What's the deal? Because if I'm going to quit my job and go back to school, all on trust, trusting someone who ran away last time, what guarantee do I have?

You could have a contract, Steve said.

Steve was stirring the clams now, and I knew he always meant well, but I had this terrible feeling that everything was falling apart again.

Yes, my mother said. A contract.

She was looking up, thinking. It will say we get to live at his house rent-free and he'll pay for school and everything else.

You can probably register the contract against his house in some way, like a mortgage, so that if he breaks the terms, you get the house.

My mother brightened at that idea, and I thought of my grandfather, in his broken car, all the windows smashed, every panel dented, thinking that his house would be next, that he'd come home one day from work after he was supposed to be retired and find she'd taken it apart piece by piece or set it on fire. I could imagine her doing that, setting fire to his house just to watch it burn.

I want this contract tomorrow, my mother said. I don't want to wait.

But you need a lawyer, Steve said.

No. I want the contract tomorrow, signed with a notary, just in simple terms easy to read. It'll say we can live in his house rent-free and he'll pay me $25,000 now and $2,500 each month, and if he doesn't I get his house, and when he dies, I get everything, his house and anything else.

Mom, I said. Please don't.

You wanted this, Caitlin. This is the fairy tale. This is how we know the prince will be good, because we have a contract like a knife at his back. In the real version of

Cinderella, there must be knives we don't see. I bet it's a sexual harassment suit. The prince, a politician, fondles Cinderella at a dance and she threatens to expose all, so he has to bring her to the castle to keep her quiet, and they make up the glass slipper thing as a cover.

You should be a lawyer, Steve said. That's some twisted shit.

Maybe I will be. Who knows. But first I need this contract. I need to know whether I'm still going to work on Monday.

My mother was pacing. She was on fire. Everything sounded like anger, like nothing had changed.

I'll write it down tonight, she said. And we'll make him sign tomorrow. Will he be at the aquarium?

I don't know, I said. It was only school days.

He'll be there. He wants to see you, so he'll be there. He wants to play family, so we'll give him the weight of a family.

But I'm going to Shalini's.

Not now. You want your grandfather, right?

Dread. I went to sleep with it and woke with it. My mother had found a new way to separate me from my grandfather. He would refuse to sign, and then everything would be his fault.

Steve helping her. They worked late into the night and again until noon.

We have to call Shalini, I said.

Quiet, my mother said. We're almost finished. She and Steve huddled together at the kitchen table around his laptop screen, proofreading.

I think it's good, he said, sitting back with his hands folded on top of his head. It's a new life. It changes everything for you.

Sorry, she said. Let me just finish reading. She was bent close to the screen, as if searching for something, her mouth open. Okay, she finally said. I think that's it. She turned to kiss Steve. Thank you.

We have to call Shalini, I said.

Okay, okay. I'll call and then we'll go print out, then the aquarium, then a notary.

And just tell him there will be a new contract, Steve said, revised after a lawyer takes a look. But I think this one is good.

I stood less than five feet from my mother and Steve, but I didn't exist. Steve didn't care that we weren't calling Shalini, didn't care what my grandfather would have to sign away, didn't care that I might lose him. Shalini, I said.

Fucking eh, my mother said. I'm calling now. She went to the phone and looked up Shalini's number. When someone answered, she explained too quickly. Something's come up, she said.

Let me talk with Shalini, I said, but my mother gestured for me to back off and then hung up.

Don't look so sour, my mother said. You're getting everything you wanted.

Then we were in Steve's pickup, a red Nissan 4x4. I crammed into one of the jump seats in the king cab, sitting sideways, my feet up on box speakers, the music loud and grinding, some sort of hard rock. *Black hole sun, won't you come, and wash away the rain . . .*

When we passed the exit for the shipping port, my mother gave it the finger. Fuck you, she yelled, and Steve grinned.

We passed the exit for Gatzert, too, and the aquarium, and not long afterward turned off and parked and the music ended and my ears were ringing. This'll be quick, Steve said. I'll just run in and print.

Is this where you live? I asked.

Yep.

I want to see.

Steve grinned. Well, it is a kind of palace, so I guess it shouldn't be missed.

Inside was like a garage, all gear everywhere. Skis and fishing poles, buckets, hip waders, bikes, helmets, ropes. A bench press taking up most of the tiny living room, a stereo with huge speakers. Groceries on the counters, not put away in the cupboards. A printer on the small kitchen table, stacks of papers, and he sat there with his laptop, my mother standing behind him.

His apartment smelled like the sea, like saltwater and seaweed and rot. A big crab pot the smelliest thing. Other nets and floats beside it.

Have you been here before? I asked my mother.

Yeah. Of course.

When?

I don't know when. A few times.

She wasn't looking at me. I went into his bedroom and turned on the light and it was more of the same, piles of stuff everywhere, including a big pile of dirty clothing, most of it black. Bed unmade, and the sheets felt damp in the cold, the heat not on. Smell of sweat and deodorant. My mother had been in here, and when was that? While I waited after school? And the day I was at Shalini's. And now she'd be able to visit whenever she wanted.

Vamos, Steve said. Bandidos. Un stagecoach waits con mucho gold. Mucho dinero.

Ai yai yai yai yai, my mother said.

They were excited, Steve waving the papers in the air.

We drove through snow and slush to the aquarium, the stereo blasting, and I hoped my grandfather would not be there. I wanted to save him from the bank robbers.

Let me go in first, I said when we had parked in the lot across the street.

We're all going in, my mother said.

Please. Let me talk with him first. Don't go in. Wait here and we'll come out. And I'll show him the contract.

Maybe we should just kill him after he signs, my mother said. That way we have the house and money and he doesn't get anything.

Sheri, Steve said.

Okay, fine. He lives. But he's still getting the best part of this deal. There's nothing we can do to make the terms bad enough.

I think it's a good idea to have Caitlin go in alone, Steve said.

Fine. I'm not dying to see him ever again anyway.

That's the Christmas spirit, Steve said.

That's what pisses me off most, that he really is getting everything just in time for Christmas.

But you also don't want to go to work on Monday.

True.

I took the contract from my mother and stepped out

into the snow. No sign of his car, but of course it wasn't something he could drive now anyway.

I hurried inside, where the staff looked surprised to see me. I was never here on a weekend.

I found him kneeling at a tank, his forehead against the glass, eye to eye with a hairy blenny, some sort of communion. Thin covering of hairs on the blenny's head, same as on an old man.

You'll never win a staring match with that fish, I said.

Caitlin. He put his arms around me, head against my stomach. Ah, Caitlin. I didn't think I'd see you today, and I waited yesterday but I guess you couldn't come.

I didn't go to school. We stayed home.

He stood up then and held my shoulders and looked at me. I'm so lucky to see you again. I thought I might not. He pulled me close and I put my arms around him.

What are those papers you have? he asked. He sounded afraid.

A contract. My mother said we can come live with you, and she'll go to school, but she wants money.

Well let's take a look. He guided me to a bench and we sat and he took the papers.

I'm sorry about your car.

It's only a car.

But you said it was the engine that would take you to the end.

It's okay. I can't read in this light, though. I have to get closer to one of the tanks. Find a bright one.

I took him to a brightly lit tank of triggers. They looked like art projects, colored with blue chalk.

The Bahamas, he said. I wouldn't mind living there. A place on the beach and go swimming with the fish.

The triggers can eat sea urchins, I said. They blow water to flip them over, then attack the underside.

When we go snorkeling, we'll have to have some sort of walkie-talkies so you can tell me about the fish.

My grandfather read the contract then, and I could see the two of us in a tropical paradise with palm trees and white sand, swimming through bright blue water with our walkie-talkies. Purple sea fans and giant green brain coral, sea anemones orange and white and triggers chalked blue. Parrot fish patterned in turquoise or red. Nurse sharks sleeping in piles on the bottom. Everything peaceful and warm and easy, the two of us just floating along.

Well, he said. I'll have no security anymore. I'll have to go back to work, which means I won't be here after school. Although maybe I can get an early shift to get out in time. They might give me that. We parted well enough.

I'm sorry, I said. She's mean.

No, no. Caitlin. I'm the one who failed. Your mother has done nothing wrong. And I'm lucky to have this chance. The contract is only money, and money is worth nothing, it turns out. All my life I was ruled by it, and finally I get comfortable enough and find out it's nothing. What matters is the chance to be with you and also to get to know your mother again. I would sign something a hundred times worse to have that chance.

So you'll sign?

Yes, of course.

I started jumping up and down. I couldn't help it. He laughed and said, That's worth three houses right there.

The wind had come up while we were inside, and the snow was blown now in gusts, clouds of it blocking all view and then clearing again. It swirled around the posts of streetlamps and signs, dust devils in white. My grandfather kept the papers safe in his coat, and he walked hunched over with his chin ducked.

My mother opened the passenger door of the pickup and looked down at us. The engine on and heat blasting.

Thank you, Sheri, my grandfather said. I'm happy to sign the papers. Thank you for this chance.

You have to sign with a notary today. And we'll have a new contract from a lawyer, and you have to sign that, too.

I'm happy to sign.

You fuck. I bet you are happy. Getting everything you want.

Sheri, Steve said.

Fine. But I'll never forget what you did. I'll never forget who you are.

I won't either, my grandfather said. Believe me. I know how worthless I am. Nobody knows it better.

I know it better.

I know I can't make it up to you, Sheri, but I'm going to try anyway. The house will go in your name now, and all the money I have will go to you and Caitlin. You'll have everything from me now, all that I am and all that I have. I can't offer more than that.

My grandfather in the snow and wind, his arms wide, offering up to a god.

Well it's not enough, she said. It will never be enough. Then she stepped down and he backed away. Get in, Caitlin, she said, folding her seat forward.

I climbed into the back.

Follow us, she told him, and hopped back in and closed the door. The side window was fogged and I couldn't see him.

That was harsh, Steve said.

Shut the fuck up, my mother said.

I could see Steve's jaw clenching. He put the truck in gear and drove slowly to the parking lot exit, looking in his rearview. That must be him, he said. A small rental.

Then let's go, my mother said.

I have limits too, Steve said.

My mother said nothing. Steve drove only a few blocks and parked outside a Mail Boxes Etc. Then we all went inside and my grandfather joined us.

My bank is closed now, he said. But Monday we can go and I'll transfer the house into your name. You're already listed on my retirement and life insurance accounts.

And when did this happen? my mother asked.

Years ago.

You've been here for years, living right in Seattle. Why now?

Sheri, I can't explain really.

Have you always been here?

No, I went back to Louisiana and lived there eleven years.

But you've been back here for eight?

Yeah. I'm sorry. I meant to be in touch with you right away, but I knew how angry you'd be.

Eight years.

Sorry to interrupt, folks, the notary said. She was clearly getting impatient. I need you to sign now if we're going to do this. Ten dollars per signature.

My grandfather signed the contract and the notary's logbook, then my mother signed. Then we waited.

You can come to the house now if you like, my grandfather said. And you can move in anytime.

Did you have another family?

No other children, no. But I did remarry in Louisiana.

And what happened to her? Did she catch a cold and you ran back here?

Sheri, Steve said.

My mother gave Steve a sharp look but held back this time from saying anything.

She left me, my grandfather said.

Was she younger?

Almost twenty years younger.

Jesus.

You don't have to confess everything, Steve said.

No, it's all right, my grandfather said. I'm not hiding anymore. I'm willing to tell anything.

You're such a hero, my mother said.

Twenty dollars, the notary said.

Steve pulled out his wallet.

No, my mother said. Make him pay.

I'm paying, Steve said, and he put down a twenty. Let's go.

So we followed my grandfather this time in his small white rental car. We drove up East Yesler Way, past my school, and kept going, turned north on 23rd Avenue past the high school, residential areas, a strip mall, a power substation, then he turned right on East Pine. Big houses, individual, better than where we lived. This is nice, I said. He turned left after one block, on 24th.

He'd better not live in a big house, my mother said. I'll kill him.

But the house is yours, whatever it is, Steve said.

I'll still kill him. Eight years, and where have I lived those eight years? Or the last nineteen years?

My grandfather turned left onto an unpaved drive. A small, beautiful house with space all around, on a big lot. Much bigger houses to both sides, but this small one was so perfect.

Wow, Steve said. A Victorian. Only one story, but a lot of character.

It was dark blue, with cream around the windows and steep roof, and a light blue door with a curved awning above, like a fairy-tale house.

Steve followed down the drive and parked beside the front steps. Another roof and bay window jutting out the side. Sheri, he said. This is good.

My mother was quiet.

My grandfather walked past and up the stairs, opened the front door and stood there waiting in the snow.

Sheri? Steve asked.

This is all happening so fast, she said. In just a few days, everything changes? Suddenly I have a house and I don't work and I'm living with my father who left?

We waited then, sitting in the cab as the air cooled. My grandfather went inside finally and closed the door. He was probably very cold by now. I wanted him to come out to the truck, but I understood why he didn't. I closed my eyes and wished I could pray, but there was no god I knew, only fish. The mola mola, perhaps, with that smaller white eye looking upward, mouth open in rapture, as my grandfather had said. A shadow form come close for a moment and then vanished again. Still there, but only felt, not seen.

Help us, was all I could think to ask. Crescent moon propelled by those great dark wings.

It's not fair to my mother, my mother said. If I walk through that door, it's like everything in the past didn't happen. All erased. And she could have been better. His leaving made her finish her life as a worse person. If he had been there, she could have been better.

Wouldn't she want you to have a better life now? Steve asked.

My mother wasn't able to answer. I put my hand on her shoulder and she reached up and gripped it tight. Then she exhaled. Okay, she said. Okay. Thank you both.

Inside were wood floors, old and refinished. Everything perfectly restored. Light blue walls edged in white, furniture with curved wood along the arms, high ceilings and a chandelier. My grandfather standing nervously in his sport coat and collared shirt.

Who are you pretending to be? my mother asked, but he didn't answer.

Did you do this yourself? Steve asked.

Yeah. I was a mechanic but became interested in carpentry just in the last few years.

The living room in front had a bay window and two cozy couches. I would sit here with Shalini. We'd be like cats in the sun.

My mother had continued on to the dining table, in the center of the small house, next to the kitchen. An old refrigerator, curved.

There are three bedrooms now, my grandfather said. I took out the central hallway and put a beam above, to make the dining room. Then I made the old dining room into a master bedroom. It has the bay window that looks out on the driveway and all the trees.

My mother walked into this bedroom and we followed. It had a king-sized bed with a padded headboard that matched the furniture in the living room, a rich tan-cream, the walls here a darker shade of blue. Open beams of the ceiling above. All clean and ready, like a hotel room. He wasn't living in this one.

You planned this, didn't you, my mother said. Three bedrooms.

I hoped, my grandfather said.

How long ago did you buy this house?

Three years ago.

So you've had us in the crosshairs for three years.

I've been wanting to contact you for eight years.

You know if it weren't for Caitlin I'd walk out right now and you'd never see me again. You knew that, and that's why you went through Caitlin first.

It wasn't really like that, so planned. I just wanted to see her, and I was afraid to see you. It wasn't a plan. We don't plan our lives out, Sheri. I did everything wrong, and if I could go back, I would. I'd plan the whole thing and get it right this time.

My mother left the bedroom and looked quickly in the others. So you've taken the smallest, she said. And what used to be the master bedroom is Caitlin's.

The first time in my new room. A huge bed with four posts in dark wood, carved. Soft cream comforter and pillows. I launched myself into the air and landed in heaven. I looked over and they were smiling, all three of them. I love this, I said. I love this bed. I love this room.

Lower ceiling than my mother's, but it still had exposed beams, an old wood floor, and one of those long thin couches for lounging if you're in a movie. The windows looked out on trees covered in snow, no neighbors visible, no piles of traffic cones or parked maintenance trucks.

I have to show Shalini, I said. Can she come over tomorrow?

Sweet pea, we don't even know yet when we're moving.

Can we move today?

I'll help, Steve said.

I'll have to give notice. We'll be paying for another month of our apartment.

I'll pay, my grandfather said. And you can move in now if you like.

Stop, all of you, my mother said. This isn't a musical. We're not all going to burst into song.

Steve grinned. My mother hit him in the shoulder, but only a love punch.

You do look happy there, sweet pea.

I love it.

Well I guess all we have to move are clothes and stuff. We don't have to move any furniture. So here's the deal, she said, turning to my grandfather. We move in today, but we don't give notice at our apartment. You keep paying rent. And you spend the night there whenever I say. If I can't stand having you here, you leave. Okay?

I was afraid my grandfather would say no, but he nodded.

That's fine, Sheri. It's your house now, and I'll leave whenever you need me to.

That's not really fair, Steve said, getting kicked out of your own house.

Anything's fair, my grandfather said. Really. Anything's fair. Just seeing Caitlin happy in her new room, that's enough.

I loved my grandfather so much right then, but I was afraid I'd get in trouble with my mother if I went to hug him. One hug could destroy all the plans.

Well, Steve said. Let's get moving.

I've never been so happy as when we drove to our apartment, my grandfather following behind. Crammed into the jump seat of the king cab, Steve's music grinding, I felt like I was glowing, my entire body some kind of sun. I kept smiling. My life was beginning again that day. I could feel it.

When we arrived, I ran up the stairs to the door. It was the only way I could hide my happiness, to run ahead where my mother wouldn't see me smile.

Steve was up the stairs next, grinning at me, and then my mother followed by my grandfather, who was carrying a suitcase.

My mother paused when she had the key in the door. I don't think I can have you in my stuff, she said. Sorry. Can you wait in your car?

Sure, my grandfather said. That's no problem. I'll leave this suitcase for you to use.

My mother had said sorry. For the first time, she had said sorry to him. It didn't matter that he'd have to wait in his car.

I saw the apartment as if for the first time, plain and cold, no warm wood, nothing cozy, all the furniture cheap, made of plywood. In the faint light, it all seemed colorless and empty, and strange that we had considered this home. We were going to live now in a different world entirely.

You can use his suitcase, my mother told me. Pack everything for a week or two, including anything you need for school. I'm not coming back if you forget something.

I didn't have much clothing. I folded my jeans and shirts carefully, and they fit into the suitcase and I still had space for everything from the bathroom. I had a separate backpack for schoolbooks. That left only stuffed animals and other toys that seemed too young for me now. Nothing was for my current age. It had been forever since we'd bought anything. I don't think I really felt poor until that moment, when I looked at all that I didn't have. I had wanted to start playing an instrument the year before, but we couldn't buy anything, and they didn't have enough at the school. They had a spare tuba, and two trumpets, but I wanted a flute or clarinet, and those were all being used. So there was no instrument to pack. I wasn't on any sports teams, because that also cost money for cleats and outfits and dues. I had my aquarium pass, and that was really it.

Can I play an instrument now? I yelled.

What? my mother yelled from her room.

Can I play an instrument now.

Just pack your stuff, Caitlin.

I brought the suitcase and backpack to the front door, then stood in the door of my mother's room. She had far more clothing than I did, accumulated through the centuries. She was stuffing it into black garbage bags.

I'm playing an instrument now, I said. Flute or clarinet. And I'm playing a sport.

Just focus, Caitlin.

I'm already packed. Because I don't have anything. I own nothing.

My mother was fast. She hooked the back of my neck. You are not going to treat me that way, she hissed, quiet enough that Steve wouldn't hear. He was hidden behind the kitchen counter, packing pots and pans into a box. I struggled for you and provided what I could. You are not going to lord over me the fact that he has more money. He supported no one. That's why he has more money. And it's my money now, so you'll behave if you want anything.

Sorry, I said.

Her face so mean and old. She finally let go, went back to her garbage bags.

At the kitchen phone, I dialed Shalini, then went as far as the cord would stretch away from Steve and my mother.

I cried, Shalini said. You made me cry, when I heard you weren't coming.

Oh, I said, and I felt this overwhelming sadness at the thought of her crying. It made my heart hurt. I'm sorry, I said. My mother did that. We're moving to my grandpa's house. You have to come there tomorrow and spend the night. He'll take us to school on Monday. I have to be quick. The address is 1621 24th Avenue, a small blue house, old and really beautiful. I have a big bed. But I have to go now. My mother can't know I'm calling.

Wait, Shalini said.

Sorry, I said. Just come tomorrow as soon as you can.

My suitcase and backpack, one box from the kitchen, and my mother's garbage bags of clothing. That was it. All that we owned, except my mother's car. We'd sell the old TV and cheap furniture.

We didn't need three cars for the move. Everything fit in our own backseat and trunk. But we followed my grandfather, and Steve followed behind us, up Alaskan Way and then angling over on East Madison, an expressway. We turned off on East Olive. His house was only a block or two away from auto stores and old high-rise apartments and the expressway, just around the corner from a YMCA, an area not much better than what we had left, but you'd never know that once you were on his street. It was tucked away just enough, and there were nice houses close to us, and all the trees that shielded us from the neighbors. A small paradise. And no planes thundering overhead at takeoff.

We parked in the driveway behind my grandfather, but my mother didn't turn off the engine. I don't know if I can do this, she said. I'm trying it for you, Caitlin. I'm really trying here. I know you've always wanted a bigger family.

Thank you, I said. I had more to say, of course, about her getting a house and my grandfather giving up everything and agreeing to everything, but I didn't dare.

And we didn't have it so bad, she said. I'm sorry you didn't get a flute. But you had everything you needed. It'll be nice to have more, but you had everything you needed.

My grandfather walked past, not daring to look at us. He went up the steps and opened the front door.

Okay, my mother said, turning off the engine. Let's see what happens.

The day cold, the sky in close, a dull gray-white, but inside the house was everything warm.

Welcome to your new home, my grandfather said and winked at me. It was just like when Charlie inherits the chocolate factory and Willie Wonka is finally friendly after being so mean, even though my grandfather was never mean. But it was that same feeling of suddenly inheriting the entire world and having endless possibility, all limits and poverty and fear gone.

I went to my room and closed the door, just so it could be

mine for a moment, only mine. Even the light was warm. A small chandelier above and a standing lamp in one corner, by the lounge. I reclined on the lounge like a Hollywood star and looked at my enormous bed and the dark beams above. This is me, I said softly. This is my life now. I was trying it on, a new life the same as a new outfit, something that changes you and you can't ever see yourself the same way again afterward. I knew this would be a moment I'd remember forever, and so I still see now exactly what the trees and sky looked like outside the windows, muted and fading and calm, without wind, and the white windowsills, a perfect milky shining white, new, and the walls not blue but papered tan in an endless pattern that shifted in light, a pattern made by texture only, silky-smooth swirls in what otherwise was a matted surface. Over the years, I would see anything and everything in that wallpaper, the walls themselves a kind of mirror, and on this first day I knew it would be that way. I knew I could fall into the walls endlessly, and the beams above, and the soft bed and comforter, and this lounge, and I knew that the wood floor, also, by being so old and having patterns of dark knots and old nail holes would shift and never be the same floor twice. A home rather than a box, and infinite what tan and cream and brown could be, as infinite as anything Charlie or any prince or princess ever knew. And someday I know I will live there again, in that same room, when my mother is gone. I want to finish there. That will be the room to take me to the end, the home given by my grandfather. He's gone now, but he left us something, a place to remember him. Every surface here finished by his own hands, dreaming of us.

But that day I was just settling in with my grandfather and thought he would live forever. I came out of my room and he was standing there smiling at me, as happy as I was about my new home.

Thank you, Grandpa, I said, and he didn't say anything but just hugged me.

My mother and Steve were putting things away in her room. My grandfather and I went to sit on the couches by the front window to wait.

Do I have any other family? I asked. Cousins or aunts or uncles?

I'm sorry, Caitlin. Your grandmother did have a sister, but I lost touch with her decades ago, and I don't know whether she ever married or had children. I don't think so. And I didn't have any brothers or sisters. We just both came from small families. When we moved here, we were on our own.

Where was she from? I asked. I loved that he would talk with me and tell me anything. My mother was never like that.

Louisiana, same as me. Seven years younger. We had no money, and only occasional jobs, and we wanted to get away. We wanted new lives. I was thirty-six and she was twenty-nine. This was the end of 1958, beginning of 1959. We didn't know how cold it would be here. We wanted somewhere no one would know us, but she got pregnant early on, so we were struggling. The freedom never really happened.

I tried to listen to everything carefully, but I don't remember all that he said. Lives so far in the past and removed, and this grandmother I always imagined as old but who had never been old.

Do you have photos of her? I asked.

Sorry, Caitlin, he said. I ran away and didn't keep anything. I tried to forget my whole life and start a new one, and it wasn't my first time doing that, either.

When was the first time?

When I left for the war. And the second time was when I came back. And then moving here to Seattle with your grandmother, that was my third time running away. And then leaving her was the fourth, and then coming back here from Louisiana was the fifth. All my life I've been running, but I promise you this is it. I'm staying this time, until the end, no matter what happens. You can count on that. I won't run away from you, ever. I know I did that day in the aquarium, but it won't happen again.

I was leaned in against him and he had his arm around me, so comfortable. I remembered the policewoman and all her questions, and I realized my mother wouldn't like seeing this either, so I straightened up and then stood as if I wanted to look out the window. I went up close to the glass and looked at the long front yard covered in snow. What war? I asked.

The big one, World War II.

You're that old? I turned and looked at him, and I just couldn't believe it. World War II is in the oldest movies, I said.

He chuckled. Yeah. A living piece of history. I was nineteen when I joined up, so I was on the young end.

What happened?

Oh, you don't want to know.

But I can't imagine anything.

I was the same as I am now, a mechanic. I worked on

diesel engines in tanks and trucks and even a few small boats. So imagine a mechanic but dressed like soldiers you've seen in the movies. None of the exciting scenes, but just a lot of mud and oil and tools and the tanks not working most of the time. War is mostly repairs and delays and always having to move again. Like the first few minutes of the movie, but repeated endlessly.

What are you talking about? my mother asked. She had appeared suddenly with Steve.

Oh, my grandfather said. Nothing. Caitlin was asking about when I was in the war. But there's nothing to tell, really. Just fixing engines.

I thought you never talked about the war. Mom always said you didn't want to talk because you had some terrible times and were all broken about it. What happened to that? Now you talk about it to my daughter, whatever she wants to know?

Sheri, I'm sorry. There were some bad times, but I try not to think about them, you're right, and I wasn't going to tell her any of that, of course.

Well it's time to tell. I want to hear. What were the bad moments?

Sheri. It's 1994. He had his arms out, indicating everything around us, an entire world. It's a Saturday. You're just settling in. We should go out to dinner. No one wants to hear about a war from another time.

I do. I want everything you never gave us before.

My grandfather had his mouth open but wasn't saying anything. How would I know where to start? he finally asked.

Start with what explains you. It should explain why you

left. Something that happened in the war or earlier in your life that made you leave, because I have to find some way not to hate you so much. I'm giving you a chance here.

There are no stories like that, no stories that can explain. I was a coward and I ran away. I did something unforgivable, and I know I can't make up for it, and I'm sorry.

That's not enough. You're going to search until you find something, and you're going to tell me. Right now.

Sheri. Please.

You do it now or we're gone. You give me some way to have some sympathy for you as I stand in this nice house, all lovingly redone, and think about the broken house you left us in, with its leaky roof and no heat and no insulation and nothing. Tell your sob story about the fucking war, whatever it was that my mom thought you were so broken about.

My grandfather closed his eyes. No story ever explains. But I'll give you what you want. I think I know the moment you want, because I made a kind of decision. There was some change. But I can't start the story at the beginning. I've never been able to do that. I have to start at the end and then go back, and it doesn't finish, because you can go back forever.

Do it, my mother said.

I don't think Caitlin should hear.

She can hear.

Okay. You're her mother.

That's right.

So I won't give the awful details, but I was lying in a pile of bodies. My friends. The closest friends I've ever had. Not piled there on purpose, but just the way it ended up because I had been working on the axle, lying on the ground. And the thing is, the war was over. It had been over for days, and we were laughing and a bit drunk, telling jokes. There was something unbearable about the fact that we'd all be going our separate ways now. The truth is that we didn't want to leave. We wanted the war over, but we didn't want what we had together to be over. I think we all had some sense that this was the closest we'd ever be to anyone, and that our families might feel like strangers now.

So that's it? You couldn't be a father and husband because you weren't done being a buddy?

No. No. It's the way it happened, in a moment that was supposed to be safe. After every moment of every day in fear for years, we were finally safe, and that's when the slugs came and I watched my friends torn apart and landing on me, dying. That's the point. We were supposed to be safe. And with your mother, too, I was supposed to be safe. A wife, a family. The story doesn't make any sense unless you know every moment before it, every time we thought we were going to die, all the times we weren't safe. You can't just be told about that. You have to feel it, how long one night can be, and then all of them put together, hundreds of nights and then more, and there's a kind of deal that's made, a deal with god. You do certain terrible things, you endure things, because there's a bargain made. And then when god says the deal's off later, after you've already paid, and you see your friends ripped through, yanked like puppets on a day that was safe, and you find out your wife is going to die young, and you get to watch her dying, something that again is going to be for years, hundreds of nights more, all deals are off. Nothing is owed.

So that's it?

My grandfather looked collapsed, sitting there on the couch with his head down and hands hanging. Yes, he said. I forgot that I owed you, that you were a child and should be given everything. I forgot that my wife was owed something, also, that my deals weren't only with god, that the deals weren't only about me. It's a terrible thing to forget. I was selfish. And I'm sorry. I have to admit, though, I do understand why I left, and I forgive myself for leaving. I guess I didn't realize that until right now, having to say all this, but I do forgive myself, or at least I understand why I did it, which maybe is the same thing.

Well, my mother said. Congratulations.

My grandfather had a grim smile, then, very strange. Yes. Congratulations. One life can never know another's.

We were at a chowder house, a fish restaurant, expensive. More expensive than any other restaurant I'd ever been to. My mother did that on purpose, I knew. She was burning through what would have become her own money, but still she wanted to punish him, and this was one way, to make him watch his dollars disappear.

Have you decided? the waiter asked. I was still panicking over the menu. There was nothing inexpensive. It wasn't like other menus. The types of fish were listed at the top, and then you could pick how it would be prepared, and pick side dishes and combinations. The menu was like a math problem, and all the numbers too high.

I'll have the king crab, my mother said. And the moonfish.

The moonfish is amazing, the waiter said. An excellent choice. It's very rare that we have it on the menu, flown in fresh from Hawaii. And it should be only lightly seared, very lightly. It has such a delicate, buttery flavor, and that's gone if you sear it a moment longer.

How much does that cost? Steve asked.

It's sixty-five dollars for the moonfish, and really the best choice we have on the menu tonight.

Sheri, Steve said.

He'll have the moonfish also, my mother said, pointing to Steve. My father is treating tonight.

Excellent, the waiter said.

I'll have the moonfish also, my grandfather said.

Did you know he's a war hero? my mother asked, raising her voice, so that others would hear, pointing to my grandfather. World War II. He watched his buddies die.

I'm sorry, sir, the waiter said quietly, and thank you for your service.

He also abandoned his dying wife. My mother still speaking in this loud voice, people looking at us. I was fourteen and got to take care of her and watch her die. Maybe not so heroic, that part. But I think we have to forgive our heroes anything, because they watched their buddies die. What do you think?

The waiter wore a small smile that was a wince. He said nothing, and for what seemed like a long time, our small side-room of the restaurant and its half-dozen tables were silent.

I'm sorry, my grandfather said. I deserve all that.

Then it was quiet again. I thought Steve would say something, defend my grandfather, but he didn't. If he had, I think he would have lost my mother right then.

My grandfather handed his menu to the waiter, then Steve did the same, and my mother, and the tables around us began talking quietly again.

And for you? the waiter asked me. His voice was barely more than a whisper, and I felt sorry for him.

I can't eat fish, I said. I love them too much.

Oh, he said, and then my grandfather said, I'm so sorry, Caitlin. I forgot. Do you have anything on the menu that's not fish?

We do have a burger, and also a simple pasta marinara.

Pasta, please, I said, and my grandfather said, Me too, instead of the fish.

My mother folded her arms and looked down at her napkin. I'm sorry, she said when the waiter had left. That was too much. I came here to punish you, and apparently to punish Caitlin, also, without even realizing it. But that's not me. I don't want to be mean like that.

Steve put his arm around her, and she leaned onto his shoulder. She was starting to cry, but careful not to make any sound. I was afraid to move, afraid to say anything, and I think my grandfather was too. So we just sat there and waited until she wiped at her eyes and sat up straight again.

What do you think you'll study? my grandfather asked, maybe just to break the silence. But it was good that he was the one to speak.

Oh, my mother said. I have to do my GED first. I can

probably take a course to study for that. Then maybe a community college for the first two years, something easy to get into, and I'd like to work hard and move on to something better for the last two years. But I don't know what subject yet.

We can do our homework together, I said.

My mother smiled. Yeah. That'll be fun, sweet pea. But your old mother is out of practice, so you'll have to encourage her. Right now, I can't really imagine doing homework.

We hadn't touched the bread, but Steve passed it around now and poured a bit of olive oil onto each of our small plates.

A dense white bread better than any I'd had before, and oil that was green and not at all like what we had at home. I love this oil, I said.

Our little gourmand, Steve said.

I just thought I might be a chef, my mother said. But then I realized they have late nights. And doctors go through endless residencies and night shifts. And lawyers have ridiculous hours also and have to fight every day. And business school leads to the biggest shark tank. Are there any jobs that don't involve giving up your life?

My hours are all right, Steve said. You can make choices. I went for less money and more free time.

The key is to escape doing labor for hourly pay, my grandfather said. I never escaped that, and I'm sorry you were stuck there, too, for so many years. Any sacrifice you make to escape is worth it, I think. How many tens of thousands of hours was I reminded of exactly what I was, standing over an engine, working with my hands. The problem was that my thoughts didn't count, and who I was didn't count, and there was no shape to any of the work. Just an endless series of engines that someone else could have fixed. It was like not being there but having to be there anyway, and that feeling from work infected the rest of my life, even though I like working on engines. It was the fact of not being free and not mattering. So I hope you'll do something that doesn't make you disappear.

Thank you, my mother said quietly. That does help. That's how it was for me too. I was there but not there.

Well you won't be going back Monday morning, Steve said. That's pretty cool.

Yeah, my mother said, but she looked overwhelmed and tired. Slumped down in her chair.

The king crab arrived then. Enormous legs white and red on a long platter, and my mother sat up.

That's a big one, Steve said.

And here's some melted butter, the waiter said, setting down a small steel cup. Enjoy. And then he was gone, out of there quickly.

We can share this, my mother said.

I can't, I said.

It's not a fish.

I know. But they're in the aquarium. I don't love them in the same way, but still I think of those legs moving, reaching up toward the glass.

Okay, my mother said. Please don't say anything more. I want to enjoy. I don't want to imagine my food moving.

My mother had a bit of a smile when she said it, though, and it felt like the weight was off us. Steve grinned and grabbed a leg and snapped it.

You can use the olive oil instead of butter, he said. Healthier, and I think it actually tastes a lot better. He poured oil onto his bread plate and my mother nodded and he poured onto hers, also, and they dipped long sections of white meat edged in red. Meat made of small strands all radiating from the center, as if the crab had been born in a burst of light, a small sudden explosion on the ocean floor, unnoticed. That's what I saw then, darkness and cold at depth and each crab winking into existence. They seemed as alien as that, not born of this world.

We all went to bed early that night. I think we were avoiding the possibility of another argument. The house quiet. My grandfather just on the other side of my bedroom wall, so close. Our heads maybe two feet apart as we slept, and I wondered whether he had done this on purpose.

My mother and Steve behind the other wall. I was in the middle, safe. I wished we could be like nurse sharks or clown loaches, just piled up together in the corner of one room, sleeping on top of each other, suspended in the one element, no separation of air, but at least we were all here under one roof and rooms touching. Only Shalini was missing.

It felt very strange to sleep in a new home. Eyes closed, snuggled under the enormous comforter, the bed so much softer than any I'd experienced before, something I could sink into, but I was trying to feel the outlines of the house, trying to reach into every corner to make it familiar. Like sonar in dolphins, closing their eyes and feeling their way through darkness, knowing shape and void. Was it a sense like touch or like sight?

And sharks, able to sense electromagnetic fields. Brains tiny and prehistoric, without feeling or memory or thought but somehow knowing the electrical weight of every living thing, even the faint movement of a fish's gills or the beating of its small, simple heart. I wanted to know this, too, to have the darkness light up with every movement and breath. I could understand it only as a kind of vision. Impossible to imagine the contact of a new sense.

I wanted to live submerged. The problem was air, too thin and cold, all contact lost. Shalini seemed forever away, unreachable, and even my mother and grandfather. The room would become solid again, walls something that could not be reached through, everything hidden, and I'd open my eyes and see only faint outlines of all that enclosed.

I finally slept, somehow, and when I awoke it was to the smell of bacon. My room cold and comforter soft and warm, and this was perfect, to hide away, smelling breakfast.

I waited until my mother knocked at my door, softly, and then opened it and peered in. Morning, sweet pea, she said. Steve made pancakes.

Mm, I said.

My mother came in and sat beside me on the bed, brushed the hair back from my face. How do you like your new home? she asked.

I love it.

Me too. It's different to live in a nice place, to look up at the dark wood beams in the ceiling. To not have everything cheap. I can't explain it, but I feel different inside, as if a nice floor and this furniture can change what I'm worth, the core of me. I know it shouldn't be like that, but I feel it anyway. A kind of warmth, or relaxing, like it's easier to breathe.

My mother no longer so hard, so mean. I wanted her always to be like this, softened and happier, but I knew her anger could come back at any moment, without warning.

Plates are on the table, Steve called out.

My mother gave me a pat on the leg. Time to get up, sleepyhead. You can just wear your pajamas and slippers.

My stomach was growling, so I was up fairly quick. It was much warmer in the main room. Steve and my grandfather and mother all sitting at the table, already started eating. I had to pee, and I loved the bathroom with its old toilet that had a water tank up high and a chain to pull with a white porcelain handle. Wood floor in here too, no disgusting carpet anywhere, and a claw-foot tub. It was a big bathroom, which was why my grandfather's bedroom was so small. A fancy mirror and slats of wood halfway up the walls.

I pulled the handle and washed my hands and looked at myself in the mirror, hair sticking up on one side from my pillow. Eyes sleepy, but I looked happy. Pale skin that seemed very thin. If I were a fish, I'd be something for a cave, pale and big-eyed and not used to light. Bones showing through. I puffed my mouth, tried to imagine gills. The sides of my jaw almost the right shape. My hair sticking up could almost be a dorsal fin, a bit lopsided. But my stomach was growling, so I needed to move out of this cave to feed.

My plate was already piled with pancakes and strawberries and bacon. Yay, I said.

Steve smiled. He liked to have his food appreciated.

This is a big step up from my usual cereal, my grandfather said.

There was a knock then, and I knew it was Shalini. I screamed and ran to the door and could hear her scream even before I opened it. We collided in a hug and jumped up and down.

I'm sorry, her mother was saying. You're having breakfast. We're too early. I told Shalini, but she demanded to come.

My mother was laughing, though. Caitlin didn't even tell us. This was arranged on the sneak.

No, Shalini's mother said. I'm so sorry. I'll take her back home.

It's fine, my mother said. It's funny.

Shalini and I were hugging, and I felt a flush of heat, and I knew we had to not do this in front of everyone, so I grabbed her hand and pulled her toward my bedroom. You have to see, I yelled. It's the most beautiful house, and the best bedroom.

I pulled her in and slammed the door shut and then we were kissing. Her soft purplish lips, so delicious. I kept looking at them and then kissing and then looking again, wanting her mouth, and she was laughing. Her eyes the darkest eyes and brightest at the same time, gold somehow in a deep dark chocolate brown.

I only think of you, she whispered. I can't think of anything else. What have you done to me?

I couldn't stop kissing her, even when she was speaking. Her hands on my back, under my pajamas, pulling me close.

Caitlin, my mother called, and knocked on the door. You have to finish breakfast. And maybe say hello to Shalini's mother. Jeez.

Maybe they'll just go away, I whispered.

Shalini smiled and stepped back, pushed my hands away, then opened the door. This is a beautiful home, she said to our smiling mothers.

Have you had breakfast? Steve asked. Please join us for pancakes, both of you.

I should go, Shalini's mother said. My husband looked very confused when we left.

Shalini's mother was beautiful. And just listening to her, you could tell she didn't have the rough side that my mother had. I wanted her to stay as a shield. My mother free to do or say anything in front of my grandfather and Steve, and this would be true in front of Shalini, also, I knew, but not her mother. Please stay, I said.

She put her hand on my cheek. How darling, she said. But I should go. Have fun, and don't stay up all night. She looked at my mother then. They haven't told you it's a sleepover, have they?

No, my mother said. But that's fine.

I'll take them to school tomorrow, my grandfather said. He was standing at the table holding on to his chair. It must have been so strange to suddenly have all these people in his home.

Are you sure? I can take Shalini back home now.

No, really, my mother said.

Well I'll leave you then, she said, and kissed Shalini's cheek and was out the door.

Well, Steve said. The most fabulous breakfast ever made by human hands is getting cold.

So modest, my mother said.

No bacon for Shalini, I said. And I have to give back my bacon, too.

More for me, my mother said, and reached over and grabbed the beautiful strips that had been on top my pancakes. I was sad to see them go.

You can have your bacon, Shalini said, and I loved the way she said it, her voice in a lilt that made the word bacon something new.

No, I said. I'm a Buddhist. I worship the golden fish.

Shalini laughed.

What's that? my mother asked. She was talking with her mouth full of pancake. My grandfather and Steve were tucking in, also, everyone's forks busy. Only Shalini used a knife to cut.

After Steve told me about the Pharaoh Fish, I told Mr. Gustafson that I was Buddhist and worshipped the golden fish.

Nice influence, my mother said, and punched Steve.

What? Steve said. I was only talking about my time in Egypt, when I lived on the bottom of the river.

Now I see why Caitlin is so crazy, Shalini said.

My grandfather looked so happy, watching us eat and talk. When I remember him, I often think of that morning, because it was our first time all together with Shalini, a wonderful morning when all was peaceful and good, no fighting, and our lives seemed like new things that would stretch on forever. An innocence. There would be such terrible moments later that day, but for now, all was safe and calm, and I could still love everyone in an easy way.

It began with Steve's idea to go cut down a Christmas tree. He should have known this would be too much for my mother. She didn't want my grandfather to have a happy Christmas family time. We all should have known to say no. But Steve looked so excited.

We'll run through the snow like wolves, he said. I'll carry the handsaw, like some man from a fairy tale. I've always wanted to do this and never have. Just run into the forest and cut down a tree.

Is that legal? my mother asked.

One tree, Steve said. And not even a big one. Who will miss it?

I don't know.

What about you, Caitlin? Steve asked. And Shalini. Do you want to run through the forest like wolves?

I looked at Shalini and we laughed.

That sounds like a yes, Steve said. What about you, Bob? he asked my grandfather.

Okay, my grandfather said. He was smiling. I don't mind getting in a little trouble. This was the end of breakfast, all of us full and leaning back into our chairs. My grandfather's arms crossed. He wore a brown cardigan. His eyes blinking.

Well, my mother said. I don't know. She grabbed a last strawberry. I guess if I have to spend the night in jail, at least I don't have to go to work right after.

There you go, Steve said. We're all set then. He jumped up from his seat and started grabbing dishes.

All the maple syrup everywhere, and I wanted to kiss Shalini with maple syrup lips.

My first Christmas tree, she said. Today I will be more American.

How long have you been here? my grandfather asked.

Six months.

How is your English so good after only six months?

We learned English in school in Delhi, where I come from. It used to be British English, so I have a bit of an accent, even though everyone's learning American now.

Fancy, my grandfather said.

Yes. I try to be fancy.

My grandfather laughed. Well any friend of Caitlin's is a friend of mine.

My mother had a sour look already, and my grandfather should have been more careful.

I got up and helped with the dishes.

What's Delhi like? my grandfather asked.

We had a bigger house, many rooms, and many people to do the cooking and cleaning, and I had tutors. And the city was enormous, and had so many things.

It seems strange that you left.

Yes.

We'll all need boots and snow pants, Steve said.

We don't have those, my mother said. Cheap rain pants, I guess, the kind you just put over your regular pants, but no boots except rubber ones.

Those'll work. We won't be out in the snow long. Just put on some good socks, two layers.

I don't have any boots, Shalini said. I'm sorry.

It's a different place, my grandfather said. But it sounds like you had everything in India, like your family was well off there.

Yes.

You have a class system there.

Yes, a caste system.

We should get moving, Steve said. I need to run to my place for the saw and my boots and such. Then we'll head off in my truck and one of the cars.

Shalini doesn't have boots, I said.

We'll grab some on the way out, Steve said. Just some rubber boots.

What caste was your family? my grandfather asked.

Khatri, Shalini said.

And what's that?

I guess it's the ruling class. My great-grandfather was a wazir.

And what's that?

The advisor to the king. The second most important person.

Holy smokes. You're royalty, or aristocracy or nobility or something.

Shalini laughed. Not really. We're just American now.

But what was it like? my grandfather asked. What was it like growing up in that class?

Jesus, my mother said. Suddenly you're the interested one. Want to know all about the world, and hear all of Shalini's stories.

Sorry, my grandfather said. I'm just curious about the other side, what it's like to grow up not struggling for money.

My father has to work, Shalini said. My family lost all of their land.

How did that happen? my grandfather asked.

Seriously, my mother said. You don't give a shit about your own daughter, and then you have to know everything about Shalini's family ten generations back.

I'm sorry, Shalini, my grandfather said. This is my fault. It's true I wasn't here.

It's not just that you weren't here, my mother said. It's also that you still don't give a shit. You like seeing Caitlin and her little friend, because how critical, really, are twelve-year-olds going to be? You get to play Santa.

It's not like that.

Really?

Of course I want to know about your life. I want to know everything. I'm just afraid to ask.

Spare me. Poor little grandpapa having to walk on eggshells around his big bad daughter.

Please, Mom, I said.

Jesus, Caitlin. You really have a way of stepping in it.

I do want to know, my grandfather said. I want you to tell me everything. The others can go cut down a tree, and you and I can sit here and talk and I want to hear everything.

Not so easy. I'm not going to just vomit up my life in one day. An occasional question would be nice. Just some small sign of interest as you do your long interviews with everyone else.

The fire had gone out of my mother. We were all looking at the floor. Just silence and no one moving. I felt so bad for Shalini, but this was a moment I couldn't do anything.

There was a clock ticking. I've always hated that sound. Unbearably tense and also empty at the same time, soulless. It seemed impossible that my mother would ever forgive my grandfather.

When we finally had the saw and all the boots and rain pants, we drove east on Interstate 90, over Mercer Island and toward nothing. My mother and Steve in the pickup, Shalini and I with my grandfather in his small rental car. The sky a white void, the clouds in low, falling of snow without wind, then clear, then falling again. Sound only of the car.

Mount Rainier somewhere off to our right, south, but invisible, Mount Baker to the left. Desert ahead. I'd never been there, and it was hard to believe, but not far ahead, within a hundred miles, all the rain and trees just ended suddenly in desert. I wanted to go there.

Shalini and I had to sit apart in the back because of the seat belts, but we held hands down low. I was afraid she'd never come over again after all the fighting. Who would want to come to my family's house a second time?

Have you been to the desert? I asked my grandfather. He hadn't said a word since we left. This wasn't like him.

Yeah, he said, sounding tired. Have you?

No. We never drive anywhere. I've never been to Canada or Oregon or Montana or anything. I haven't even been out to the islands.

Well. We have to change that.

Then he was silent again. Sound of the engine and tires, Shalini holding my hand but looking out her window into the blankness. The car cold. He hadn't put the heater on. I was bundled up but could feel my nose and ears.

What's the desert like?

My grandfather sighed, then waved one hand in the air. It's uh, like the moon. You leave the forest and go to the moon in about one mile, like two planets were cut in half and then stuck together. Suddenly there are no trees. Sorry, I just don't feel like talking.

Why?

Your mother will always hate me. That's what I think now. I don't think it will change. I guess I let myself believe she only needed time, but I don't believe that now.

She doesn't hate you.

Each thing that happens to us, each and every thing, it leaves some dent, and that dent will always be there. Each of us is a walking wreck.

I squeezed Shalini's hand, and she squeezed mine back

and looked over, sad and afraid. There were no limits to what could happen in my family.

Trees like ghosts out of the white, so still and straight and waiting in silence, all of them, hundreds, with only empty gaps between, a forest cold and abandoned. My grandfather drove on past small gravel roads leading to parks and lakes until the slope rose into exposed black rock that disappeared in cloud. The higher forest, and it seemed we might just drive forever and become lost, and that this might be a good thing, but Steve finally pulled to the shoulder where the trees huddled in close, and we all piled out into the cold.

I don't like this forest, I said.

Steve nodded. Frosty, he said. He must be living nearby. Not wearing a nice scarf and hat but only snow and a stick nose and eyes from small stones, and he's hiding behind trees and watching, and he's not alone. There are others like him, other snowmen.

Stop, my mother said. You're going to scare them.

But Steve came and took my hand and Shalini's. If you see anything, he said in a quiet voice, just run.

I looked at Shalini, both of us terrified, and then Steve laughed. Don't worry. How fast can a snowman run?

He grabbed a long saw then with big teeth and stepped into the forest, really like some man in a fairy tale, a brown scarf around his neck, brown jacket and pants, same color as wool spun in a village of small houses made of logs. A fire in every hearth to keep out all that lurked, all the houses arranged facing each other in a tight circle, and this man walks out alone.

But my mother followed, and then my grandfather, and Shalini and I were too terrified to stay behind, so then the trees were swallowing us too.

Shalini's hand squeezing mine tight. Her face faded already from cold, turned ashen, as if we could walk here and become as bloodless as the snowmen. I was looking everywhere for them, at the edge of every tree, behind every snowbank. Small black eyes and stick nose all that we'd see, the larger outlines lost in all other white. Eyes and nose enough to imagine evil, all that's needed for a face.

Sound of our rubber boots squeaking against the snow, so loud, drawing all of them near. I saw them shifting through trees faster than anything with blood could run, and I thought maybe they could hear blood, could hear our hearts beating, looking for warmth, needing it, come to carve out our still-beating hearts.

I screamed and ran, and Shalini screamed, and we charged through the snow, still holding hands, pushing away branches, stumbling and rising again, the sky the same as the snow, all white and blinding, and every tree hiding something, and we could never outrun ourselves.

We fell into a hollow under a large tree, deep into the snow, buried past our waists. Trapped and whining now with fear, no longer screaming, clutching at each other, looking everywhere, to all sides, expecting to see the snowmen rushing in. Exactly like sharks, invisible in their element, shadows and phantoms felt shifting and sensing the beating of your heart, and you want to believe they're only imagined, and then suddenly it's too late and you're devoured.

I felt trapped in that hollow, tried to climb out but there was nothing to hold on to, only snow I kept sinking through.

We can't get out of here, I whispered, panicked. We're buried.

Shalini fighting at the snow, also, but we had these cheap rubber boots and rain pants that slipped, and we didn't know what to do.

Caitlin! I could hear my mother's voice, but muffled and distant, and not quite right.

Your mother, Shalini said.

It might not be her, I said. It might be a trick.

Shalini looked so scared. We listened and heard other voices now, too, that might be my grandfather and Steve or might not. Twig noses and soulless eyes, the snow itself come alive and hunting, sending voices into the forest like bait.

Don't answer, Shalini said in a voice hardly even a whisper. Don't answer, Caitlin.

We clutched at each other and tried to be silent and invisible, shivering in snow that reached almost to our shoulders. A numbness in my legs, the cold a kind of weight that took over flesh. Like a spider's web, this hollow, and the cold a poison, slow, the snowmen reaching with fingers you could never feel, only some dull recognition that all was already given over. The blood in us cooling, and it would stop soon, and we'd have only our eyes left moving without a heartbeat, to see when they came for us.

Caitlin! I heard, and I could tell it was not my mother's voice, not real. It was only the voice I wanted, worried about me, wanting to keep me safe, desperate with love. A voice to lure, but I kept silent. I knew it wasn't possible.

Caitlin! As if I were all that mattered, and this is what the snow offers, a numbing and fading of the rest of the world until you're all that's left.

My grandfather's voice too, high now and strained, not like him at all, sounding almost like a woman, old, or the high scree of sticks when they rub together in wind. The trees in collusion with the snowmen. Shalini and I pressed in close to the tree, rough bark, sharing our last warmth, but these bare lower branches around us curved in to form a thin cage. Sticks brittle but so many of them.

And then we heard footfalls, coming fast, the snowmen grown legs like wolves to travel faster, half element, half beast, water and air fused to blood, leaping at us from every direction, and we shrank down until our faces were in the snow, and we were almost fully hidden, and this was our only hope, that they wouldn't see us, but then it was Steve, panting hard, and he collapsed to his knees. They're here! he yelled. I found them!

He lay down on the snow and edged close enough for us to reach his hand. Caitlin, he said. Grab my hand. And hurry. Your mother can't see this. She'll kill me.

Shalini first, I said.

Okay. Shalini then.

I could feel Shalini shaking from cold and fear, and I let her go as Steve pulled her free, one of her boots missing. I ducked down to find it, lost inside the snow, hard grains against my cheeks.

I could hear Steve saying something but muffled, and then I found the boot and stood and could breathe and hear clearly again.

Take my hand, he said, and he pulled me sliding free. We all stood then, and he put Shalini's boot back on, and took us by the hands and we ran away from anything my mother might see. Over here! he was yelling.

The forest not yet returned to anything normal. Like a dream you can't wake from, and I think fairy tale is always waiting for us, that we can slip at any moment into forests and wolves and voices luring and believe in the shadow world. All that we fear embodied, all pattern and shape that hides somewhere within set loose.

My mother crushing me in a hug, her breath fast and hard. Have you lost your mind? You can't do that. You can't just run away into the snow.

I couldn't see her face, and she could have been anyone. How do we know to trust any form?

Steve was just being an idiot, sweet pea. There are no snowmen. Come here, Shalini, she said, and then Shalini was mashed into the hug, the three of us standing in the snow while Steve and my grandfather waited at the edges, both probably in fear.

I'm sorry, Steve said. I just thought it would be funny. I didn't know you could believe it. Frosty as some kind of evil clown. He's just Frosty the Snowman.

Stop, my mother said.

He's got a button nose, I think, not even a stick one.

I could see snowmen again, their stick noses and some with eyes not of stone but of buttons, larger and black and shiny.

Jesus, my mother said. Shut the fuck up about Frosty.

I'm just trying to say he's not scary. He's got his stick hands poking out saying hi. Steve laughed then. Okay, I'm sorry. That was too much. I just can't stop, though. You have to admit it's funny they ran from the snowmen.

Wow, my mother said, letting go of us. It's really still funny for you.

Sorry, Steve said, but he had a grin. Sometimes a Frosty will have two heads and one can come off and roll around on its own.

I didn't think to follow their tracks, my mother said. That's how panicked I was. I just ran anywhere. And after doing that, running in circles, where are the tracks then? I could have lost them.

But we didn't.

Yeah, my daughter and her little friend haven't died, so it's all okay.

Sheri. That's a bit extreme. They're okay, and they'll laugh about this later.

Ha ha, my mother said. We're going home.

Just let me get a tree.

They're shivering. Hurry up.

Steve looked into the trees, all too large, an old forest. Let's try along the road, he said. There are smaller ones there, I think, and I'll just top one.

My mother held our hands as we walked back to the road. I was still looking around, and now not only for full bodies but for heads on their own, large snowballs that would roll to the side and reveal a face.

My grandfather walking just ahead in an old wool army coat, pea green, and a hat with earflaps. A heavy form through the snow, clearing the way, like some guardian, making everything safer.

I had snow down both boots, icy and hard against my shins. This is the farthest I've ever been from home, I said. Ever.

No, Shalini said.

It's true. I've never gone anywhere. This is the farthest.

That's embarrassing, my mother said. For me. Don't ever tell anyone that again. And we'll go places now.

You've really never been anywhere? Shalini asked.

No.

You have so much to see. We have relatives in Geneva and Nairobi and Connecticut and Sydney. Every place is so different. My mother speaks five languages.

Well you're with a bunch of hicks now, my mother said. Welcome to America, where we speak American and that's it. Sorry to disappoint. I can promise you I know nothing at all about the larger world. I've worked and I've stayed here. My plans have never been more than a week in advance.

I hope you'll see Europe, my grandfather said, taking a quick glance over his shoulder. And I should have gone back, in peacetime. I know it's changed, but I'd like to go back.

Well, my mother said.

What happened when she died? my grandfather asked. What happened right after? How old were you and where did you stay? I know I have no right, but I've worried about this, over and over. If you were still under eighteen, how did you survive, and what happened to her? Was there a funeral? Was there any money for a funeral?

My grandfather had stopped and turned around, facing my mother, standing there in the snow with his arms hanging. My mother stopped also.

You don't get to ask about that time.

You said earlier today you wanted to be asked. All the way driving here I was thinking it was over, that you'd never forgive me. But then I realized you were just saying you wanted to be asked. You wanted me to show some interest. And Sheri, you'll always be the person I love most in this world. I failed, I abandoned you, but I still loved you and thought of you every day. And I need to know how bad it got. I need to know how bad I was. I need to know the end of that or I'll always imagine it worse.

It was worse. It was worse than you imagine.

Tell me then. I need to hear.

I don't owe you that.

I know, but tell me anyway. Give us a chance. How can we get along if the most important part isn't known?

My mother looked over to where Steve was climbing a tree with his saw. Not too big a tree, maybe twenty-five feet, and all of it pulsing each time he pulled upward. Branches moving in unison like a sea anemone in current.

I can't, my mother said. Because when she died, it wasn't in the hospital. There was no help. She was just in her bed, and I was only sixteen, and there was no money by then.

Tell me.

You weren't there. That's the main part.

I know.

And there was no phone by then, or electricity, and we hadn't paid rent, and there was not a single dollar.

What did you do?

I left her there, in her bed, for a long time. I just left her.

How long?

I don't know. Maybe four or five days or something. I can't be saying this in front of Caitlin.

What did you do after the four or five days? Did you call someone, or did someone come?

No one came. We had dropped off the edge of the world. We didn't pay rent, but no one cared about that, even, it was such a shitty place. And it was cold, snowing. That might have been why no one came. But there was no heat in the house, so she didn't smell any worse than before. She could have stayed right there through the winter. I thought about that, about just leaving her. I thought about hitchhiking and going somewhere else.

Why didn't you?

I don't know.

There was a loud splintering, and we all looked over at Steve as he clung to the trunk and the part above him fell away, a slow and cushioned fall twisting and dusted in white, and what remained of the tree open now to the sky.

No need to rush over and help, Steve yelled. The snowmen can help if I need it.

I danced, my mother said. That's the part you're looking for. That's how I bought food and started paying rent again and got the electricity turned back on.

You danced?

Yeah, the strip club that was close to us on the highway, Don's. That's what you wanted to hear, right? How low I went?

No. It isn't like that. I want to know because I care, because I'm sorry, because it's all my fault and what I have to make up for.

You can't make up for it. I was sixteen and showing my cunt to truckers. How are you going to make up for that?

My grandfather just stood there with this awful grimace on his face and his eyes closed. His arms in close like he was hugging himself, but hands clawing. We watched him, a shape of suffering. Waiting there in the snow together, waiting for what? What could ever help us? Sound of Steve dragging his tree through the snow. We can vamonos, he said. Caballeros.

Shalini and I rode again with my grandfather, following Steve and my mother and the Christmas tree. It poked out over the tailgate and moved like fur in the wind. Snow falling more heavily now, the world whited out and passing at high speed, flakes curving midair and sucked into our windshield as if we were a magnet, as if we had gained a tremendous and impossible weight.

My grandfather wasn't speaking. Shalini silent also, looking out the side window. I was far away from both of them, shivering and wet, my feet and hands and face very cold. I closed my eyes and ducked my chin into my jacket, tried to scrunch down and make myself small.

My mother dancing. It wasn't something I could believe. I wanted to go back to when I didn't know this. Naked in front of truckers, dancing around a pole, men throwing money at her, like in R-rated movies. And did she have sex with them? It was all too much to understand or even think about, and it was the risk that frightened me, the exposure, knowing my mother had not been safe, and fearing that somehow for myself, even though I wasn't exposed. Shame, also. Strange how easily it moves from one person to another. I felt dirty, embarrassed for Shalini to see me now.

And my grandmother lying in her bed dead for four or five days. That was too much also. All of it was too much. And what happened after? Was there ever a funeral? Was she ever buried?

The drive was too long, and not a single word spoken. When we arrived, my grandfather turned off the engine and sat there with his hands still gripping the wheel, staring straight ahead, as if we had entered some other kind of road, first heading out. But then his head bowed and he leaned forward and just hung across the wheel.

My grandfather weeping, a small sound, choked and hidden, his back shaking. I opened my door and stepped out into the snow, and then I walked around and opened Shalini's door so she could escape. She didn't look at me as she climbed out. We walked up to the porch and stood there cold and waiting. My mother and Steve in the closed pickup talking.

I'm sorry, I told Shalini.

I don't like it, she said, but it's not your fault. I'm cold, though. I need a hot bath. Do you have a key?

No. I put my arms around Shalini to try to warm her, and she ducked her head against my shoulder. There was a wind now, not much but icy. Snow reaching in under the small awning. Some fairy tale on pause, the cottage door never opening. Characters gone to the wrong place, the wrong story. Little Red Riding Hood finding herself at the houses of the Three Pigs. A wolf out there somewhere but not the right wolf, and the pigs asleep and don't hear Little Red knocking, or maybe it's the Three Bears who are sleeping in these houses now. We never know what will happen next, our lives unshaped.

So we stood shivering on that porch and waited while two other stories continued without us, my grandfather in his car recognizing finally the cost of his leaving, mourning deaths from long ago, and my mother in Steve's car. Were they talking about the snowmen, or her past, or something else?

We had been forgotten, and cold only becomes more bare, our clothing thinning. Shalini's teeth chattering, so I let go and ran down the steps to pound on Steve's door. We're freezing! I yelled.

Steve opened his door, and then my grandfather did too. I'm sorry, he said. I'm sorry, Caitlin. I forgot I'm the only one with the keys. His eyes swollen and red and wet. He hurried to the door and let us in and I took Shalini to the bathroom and ran the water for the tub and also the hot tap in the sink so we could warm our hands.

Don't make the water too hot, my mother said. You have to be careful. Start with only lukewarm.

What I imagined was that our hands could shatter, as if we were made of glass, and my fingers felt like that in the warm water, needles and shards breaking free and clogging in my veins, poking at the walls.

This hurts, Shalini said.

It doesn't last long, I told her. It'll be worse, though, in our feet. I can't feel my toes.

Nice idea, Steve, my mother said, but I don't think he heard. He was huffing and puffing and nearly knocking the house down as he brought in the tree. It had grown since we'd left the forest, enormous now. My grandfather standing helplessly by, still in his coat, watching his floor and walls scraped.

My mother tested the water in the tub and then began stripping us, boots and jackets and snow pants first, then thinking to close the door so Steve and my grandfather wouldn't see. The air warm and steamy, and I felt sleepy. I loved being undressed by my mother, just putting my arms up for her to pull off my shirt. She hadn't done this in so long.

She pushed my pants and panties down, and I stepped free and watched as she stripped Shalini. Her beautiful skin and long black hair. Small triangle of her softest hair. I looked down at my own hair that had only recently appeared, so light in color it was possible not to notice it, like the hair on my arms that you'd never see unless it was summer and the skin turned dark enough and the hairs turned golden, all curved in the same pattern.

We stepped into the tub and my toes were splintering and I could tell from Shalini's face that hers were doing the same.

Sit down, both of you, my mother said. You look dizzy.

This huge claw-foot tub, a heavy cascade of water, and as we sat, the water that burned my toes felt cold between my legs. It's cold, I said.

I'll turn it up now, slowly, my mother said, and she adjusted and tested and adjusted again as our feet thawed. You get chilblains if you go too fast, she said. Never go straight into hot water.

What are chilblains? Shalini asked.

I don't know, my mother said. But you can get them if you don't do this. And they're bad.

Shalini hugging herself, as if we were still standing on the porch, until the water rose high enough and hot enough that she relaxed. My mother bent over the tub between us, swirling the water, and the two of us naked and looking at each other, waiting for her to leave. Shalini's eyes.

It seemed like forever before my mother left us and closed the door. We met in the middle, our knees touching underwater, and had the softest kisses. Our faces damp in the steam, hair stuck to our cheeks. My spine lifting out of my back and making the rest of me curl. I couldn't believe how silky her lips were, and I slid along them and closed my eyes and thought this was so perfect.

Did you find the shampoo? my mother asked as she came in. My arms jerked back from around Shalini, lightning-quick movement of shame and fear but not fast enough.

What are you doing? My mother's voice a whisper.

I couldn't answer. Her face looked disgusted. I'll never forget that. I'll never be able to, and I'm not sure I'll ever forgive her.

Shalini had collapsed down into the water, hiding, but I remained upright on my knees and just could not believe my mother's face, all love gone and only disgust, looking at me as if I were garbage.

No, my mother said. No. You are not going to do this to me.

What's wrong? my grandfather asked, and then he looked in, and I covered my chest with my arms, sank down lower. What happened? he asked.

Stay out of this, my mother said.

But what is it?

My mother's mouth hanging open in some vicious look, and I didn't want to love her less, but I did from that moment on. Something I felt for her died right then, so quickly I don't really understand.

You have to tell me, my grandfather said, his voice rising. What the hell is going on?

What's happening? Steve asked, ducking his head in.

They were kissing. They were making out in the bathtub.

Really? Steve asked.

My mother turned her rage on Steve. Don't sound interested. You will never see me again.

Jesus, he said, and he slipped away.

I thought someone was hurt, my grandfather said. I thought something terrible had happened.

And this is not terrible, that your granddaughter is turning into a little dyke?

Sheri. Slow down here. Caitlin and Shalini are both good

kids. If they've kissed, maybe they're a little confused or something, but they haven't done something wrong.

I won't raise a pussy licker. Shalini, get out of the fucking tub right now. You're going home, and you're never seeing Caitlin again.

Sheri! my grandfather yelled, and I could see him as a father for the first time.

But my mother ignored him. She stalked over and grabbed Shalini by the hair and yanked her out of the tub, dripping and naked and grabbing at my mother's arm, trying to free herself.

Stop it! I screamed, and I was out of the tub but fell on the slick wood and was too slow. They were clogged at the doorway, my mother trying to get through, pulling Shalini, and my grandfather blocking as if this doorway led to somewhere important, as if this were the gate that had to be guarded. He had grabbed my mother's shoulders but was pushed back into the living room.

The violence has to stop, Sheri. You're violent, and it's not okay.

I'll show you violence, she said, and she punched straight ahead with her right fist. Something I could hear, and he caved, punched right in the heart. He let go of her and took a few steps backward and then just sat on the floor, collapsed. His mouth open, unable to get a breath.

I didn't know who to run to, my grandfather on the floor or Shalini with her hair twisted in my mother's fist. Shalini crying and wet and naked, exposed, and I went for my mother's arm and bit down through her shirt and into flesh. It seems so animal now, but everything about that day was barbaric, and how else could I get her to let go? I wasn't strong enough for any other way.

My mother hit me very hard then, in the face, a popping sound in my head and the world closing, and I fell back onto the floor and somehow didn't pass out. I saw my mother let go of Shalini and come to me, touching me, her face in close, sorry, but Shalini pushed her out of the way and held my head in both hands and kissed me.

How do you recover from a day like that? My grandfather on the floor trying to breathe, Shalini and I naked and wet and both hurt, my mother crawled away into her own corner, Steve hiding. How do you put a family back together, and how do you forgive?

Caitlin, my mother said. My baby. I'm sorry.

She was tucked against the wall at the end of the couch, her hands up to her face, hiding her mouth. Hands in fists like a boxer defending. She seemed animal. The fact that she could talk didn't seem to fit at all. I watched her as I would something at the zoo, removed for the first time, distant.

My grandfather leaning back propped on his hands, as if he were lounging on the grass or at the beach, but his eyes were closed and his mouth looked like pain. I don't think I had a heart attack, he said. I think I'm okay.

Someone needed to help us, all of us. Someone needed to help my grandfather up, and check my face, and dry off Shalini and put her in clothing, and somehow take care of my mother. But Steve had vanished, still hiding somewhere in the kitchen or a bedroom, failing to appear, and there was no one else.

My face was sore but strangely not broken and not even very painful. That popping sound must have been my mother's hand. Shalini so gentle, fingers on my cheek and then kissing me again.

I just can't watch that, my mother said. You don't know what it's like. None of you know. I wasn't even a dyke, but I've been called one plenty of times, working construction. And called a muff diver on stage when I danced with another woman. Men love the idea of two women together. They want to watch and then kill. You'll be hated all your life.

I think the world is different now, my grandfather said. I think they'll be okay.

You don't know anything. And I can't watch it. I won't have it in my house. Shalini is going home now. I'm sorry about what I did. But Shalini is going home now, and she's never going to come over again, and I don't want Caitlin to see her at school.

My grandfather heaved forward onto his hands and knees and then stood. He walked to the kitchen table and I could see Steve back there, standing with his arms crossed and one hand to his mouth, looking afraid.

Matches, my grandfather said, and he pulled open a drawer. This is a box of matches. He lit one, a flick and flash, and then turned to the table and lifted the contract, and he brought it over the sink and lit the lower corner and held it up as the flame grew and devoured. There's your contract, he said. Notarized and burned. And the house is not going in your name tomorrow. I don't care anymore what you think of me, or whether you'll ever forgive me. All I care about now is protecting Caitlin and Shalini. So you have a choice. If you want this house, if you want to go back to school and stop working your job, you'll let me take you tomorrow to find some help. Some counseling. I'm sorry I wasn't there to protect you, but I'm going to protect Caitlin and Shalini now, and Shalini can stay here tonight if she wants, and she'll always be welcome. And she and Caitlin can do whatever they want. It all looks like love to me.

My mother still tucked against her fists, and I thought she would explode out of there, tear my grandfather into pieces for what he'd done, but she wasn't moving.

I think he's right, Sheri, Steve said. And I'll help you too.

My mother's mouth twisted like she was going to cry, and I felt so sorry for her but also a new coldness, something I never would have imagined possible.

My grandfather came to her, knelt on the floor and put his arms around and held her close. She put her arms around him and they just stayed like that, rocking a bit. I knew both would have their eyes closed, and knew that finally they had met again. Maybe this is as near as we can come to forgiveness. Not the past wiped away, nothing undone, but some willingness in the present, some recognition and embrace and slowing down.

Shalini's skin felt cold, and I was shivering, so I sat up, my head pulsing, and we went back to the bathtub, slipped into the warmth and submerged. I closed my eyes and went all the way under and just hung there in a void because too much had happened. I heard the faucet and felt water cold then hot, and the temperature rose and I was lost in the sound of all that water, reaching like a goldfish to the surface with my lips for a quick gulp of air and then back down, returning to nothing. Shalini's hands on my legs, some caress from another world, from darkness, gentle and reassuring. The end of terrible days, the end of being afraid, the end of being alone, and I knew it, even as it happened. The end also, though, of loving my mother in the same simple, full way. The limits of my own forgiveness.

I stayed under as long as I could, not wanting to return to air or words, but the heat drove me to the surface, and then Shalini's lips, and it was the most perfect love I've ever known. No one will believe that, because we were too young, but we were absolutely there, not partially gone as adults always are. I had all of Shalini. Nothing was withheld. And she was far above me, in class and family, intelligence and sophistication and knowledge and beauty, and we didn't yet consider those things, and I couldn't yet feel inadequate in the adult way, really, even in the terrible shame of that day.

And so nothing in me was withheld either. And there was the freedom of permission for the first time. On the other side of the door they knew what we were doing, and it was okay.

The house was silent when we emerged, only one light on, over the kitchen table, all the rest darkness. Three pizzas, mostly eaten, left out for us, so we sat wrapped in our towels, the air cold but our bodies still shielded by warmth from the bath. My family hidden away, no dinner together, contact too much. The Christmas tree lying on its side along a wall. We were starving, and we finished every piece.

The comforter cold when we first slipped under, so we clung together for warmth. My own room become our room, and my family let us sleep together without shame. Sometimes the worst moments can lead to the best.

That night was perfect and the beginning. Shalini sleeping on top of me, the warmth and weight of her, the fan of her hair making a cave around my face, rise and fall of her breath and small twitches as she slept. She abandoned herself to sleep, and I was held finally to the bottom of the ocean, as I had always wanted, thousands of feet down and the two of us gliding on great wings.

My mother in the morning shy and awkward, and this was something new, something that would go on for years and never quite end, the loss of her confidence as she tried to come to terms with her anger. Rage was what had held her together for so long.

But she put out bowls for our cereal, brought spoons and milk, and tried even from that first morning, though she couldn't look us in the eye and we wouldn't have wanted it anyway. Her hair unbrushed and not pulled back, and she hid within it.

I don't know why I couldn't just forgive her completely and immediately. Or later, when I would find out no one knew about her mother's death for two years. Completely alone for that time. But something had hardened in me, some animal and instant response when I saw her disgust, how she looked at me when she first knew who I was, and some response also to being hit. A change in those moments, some switch turned off forever, the end of trust or safety or love, and how do we ever find the switch again?

So I admire that she could love her father, because I think that is what happened, and they lived here together even after I left for college. They lived in peace, and Steve remained, also, the three of them sharing a roof, and when my grandfather died, he was loved and forgiven. I'm grateful to her for that, and I hope eventually to be able to offer the same to her.

That morning, he took us to school, and he had become more like a parent. Your mother's going to be okay, I remember he said. I see now that he had learned not to run and was even discovering he was stronger than he had thought. I'll take you both to the aquarium today, he said. I'll call your mother, Shalini, and let her know.

Thank you, Mr. Thompson, she said, and she squeezed my hand.

You won't believe the fish, I said.

The whole world is in those tanks, my grandfather said. Everything.

We weren't driving on East Marginal Way. We were on residential streets, going slowly. And so much later in the morning, only a few minutes before class, the sky already white-gray, as bright as it would become.

All the cars out front, and it was my first time not entering alone, and we had only a half week before vacation. Mr. Gustafson had given up completely. The classroom was mayhem. As he gazed at his book of old cars, slouched over his desk in his Santa hat, with his tongue just protruding, the Chinese New Year dragon was winding around the chairs, weaving in and out and pulling the sleigh. Shalini and I trotted our reindeer behind with the others, and somehow there were always strips and balls of newspaper in the air and other things thrown, balloons and glue. I was hopping as we trotted Lakshmi Rudolph, and Shalini was laughing, and I wanted to kiss her, so I tried, but she ducked away. Not with people looking, she yelled, still smiling.

What would have happened if I had just kissed her anyway, right then, and kept doing that every day and never stopped until it was normal for everyone to see, even her family? But you can't go back, and I don't regret anything with Shalini. There's no point to regret.

By the time my grandfather picked us up after school, our faces were painted and there was glue on our clothes and our hair wild and we were flushed and exhausted.

Wow, my grandfather said. School is nothing like I remember it.

It's not like India, Shalini said.

Mr. Gustafson is a bad teacher, I said.

You get some like that, my grandfather said. But don't let them slow you down. Make sure you get good grades so you can go to college.

I wanted to ask my grandfather whether they had found help for my mother today, but I was afraid to ask. My cheek was bruised and sore but hidden by face paint which I would leave on for the next two days until vacation. I was afraid Evelyn would see and come around to destroy everything just as it was getting better.

We drove the route I had always walked, toward the low dark water of the sound, and we arrived so quickly.

I was holding Shalini's hand as we entered. You have to see the splendid mandarins, I said. They look like your mother's scarves.

My grandfather bought tickets for himself and Shalini, and then we ran to the first saltwater aquariums, where the most common fish lived, the ones you see in dentists' offices. Coral and anemones and these fish that looked made of silk.

They look like hummingbird frogs, Shalini said.

Everything here looks like something else, my grandfather said. These to me look like burglars, with masks on so we won't recognize them.

They're so sweet, Shalini said.

They always have that same pattern on their backs, I said. It can be a turquoise background with orange squiggles or an orange background with blue squiggles, but always the same squiggles.

My grandfather was looking around at the other mandarins now, his face so close he was almost touching the glass. You're right, he said. It's almost the same pattern. It looks so random, but they all have two circles on their backs, one forward and a bigger one farther back. Each one a little bit different but following some blueprint somewhere. As if each of us might have a blueprint. As if somewhere there's the shape of my life, and I had the chance to choose a few variations, but not far from the pattern.

I remember he said that, because I've thought of it ever since, the idea that we don't stray far, that what feels like discovery is only the revealing of what was hidden but there, waiting. I remember because I think this might be a path to forgiveness, to realize that no matter how violent, how frightening my mother was, it was not random but at least partly inescapable, that who she was had been set in motion long before and she had to suffer that person as much as I did. And the moment she looked at me in disgust, as if I were a monster, was something she was powerless to hide, because she was overwhelmed. When I think back on all that happened that day, I try to remember she was at a breaking point, try to remember back to before my grandfather appeared, before she was put under such pressure, when we'd arrive home and she'd collapse on her bed and let me collapse on top of her and I clung to her like a frogfish, my hands and feet tucked under, the soft strong mountain of her beneath me, and it felt like we were all the world.